LINGERING TOUCH

Other Works
CRAFTING A WRITER'S LIFE: Building a Foundation

Coming Soon

The Blades of Janus
PERIHELION

The Department of Homeworld Security
Nothing to Declare

Resident Alien

The Department of Homeworld
Security
Book Two

Cassandra Chandler

Copyright Page

Resident Alien
The Department of Homeworld Security, Book Two
Copyright © 2016 by Cassandra Chandler
Print ISBN: 978-1-945702-33-4
Digital ISBN: 978-1-945702-21-1

First eBook edition: April 2016
Second eBook edition: April 2017
First print edition: December 2018
10 9 8 7 6 5 4 3 2 1

cassandra-chandler.com
P.O. Box 91
Mission, Kansas 66201

Dedication

For Allie S.—a great listener.

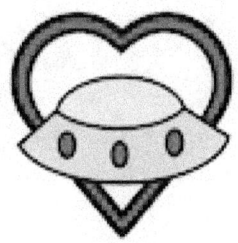

*Don't miss out on any of the alien action.
Subscribe to Cassandra Chandler's newsletter at
cassandra-chandler.com!*

Chapter One

"Greetings, my fellow interstellar travelers. This is Brendan Sloan, speaking to you from the little blue marble third from Sol. Without context, that doesn't give you much of a clue as to where I am, but if you're advanced enough to pick up this signal, I'm betting you can trace the source."

Brendan picked up the toy rocket that he kept on his desk and fidgeted with the stabilizers on its base. His stomach was full of butterflies—not the good kind—from his conversation with his sister, Paige.

She had been scheduled for a flight out of Louisiana earlier that day, but ran late at a cleanup site her environmental restoration team was working on. The plane had crashed. No survivors.

He felt terrible for the people who had been on board and for their families. And at the same time, he was grateful beyond measure that his baby sister had been spared. He was still having trouble wrapping his head—and his heart—around the situation.

"I'm keeping it short today, as I have something of a date." He hoped that Kira was listening. He needed to talk to her immediately—to hear her voice and know that she was okay as well. He spoke his mind, eager to finish the transmission.

"Humans have a need to bond. We bond with a partner, with our friends and family. With comrades-in-arms and comrades-in-ideas. It's part of what makes us strong as a species and something I hope our cultures will share. And if not, perhaps we can teach each other and grow through our own interactions."

He set the rocket down in front of a picture of him and Paige. He had his arms around her shoulders and was hugging her tight. Her expression was equal parts amused and annoyed.

They had the same blue eyes and red hair, same smile and scientific curiosity, but what they each added to the world was so different. She fought for the planet, hands on —often from the inside of a hazmat suit. Trying to get people to stop damaging their homeworld.

He worked with the government to create technology that was decades ahead of anything on Earth—tech that was supposed to be used to improve everyone's lives, but was usually turned into weapons to use against others. Hence his hiatus from his most recent project.

He ran his hands over his face, careful not to knock his headset out of place, then let out a sigh and leaned back in his chair.

"I look up at night and my eyes show me a sky filled

with thousands of stars. My instruments let me know there are so many more out there, galaxies full of them in an infinite universe. And my reason tells me this—we cannot be alone. This is my official request to parlay. Please come in peace."

It was a silly dream and a waste of time—sending transmissions into deep space in the hopes that he might get lucky and reach an alien civilization, maybe hitch a ride and find a more peaceful home. But it kept him distracted from the problems on Earth and how very little he had been able to change anything. Yet.

Time and distance would help him come back to the communications project he was working on refreshed and with new perspective. Maybe he'd even figure out how to use their results to benefit all of humanity instead of only the people he worked for.

And thanks to taking time off, he had met Kira.

Officially, Brendan had been told that Eric was his *liaison*. Eric checked in with Brendan once a month. Their conversations were superficial, but Brendan was sure Eric was under pressure from his superiors to get Brendan back on the project. Eric knew Brendan needed a break and more time to unwind. Brendan was pretty sure that was why they had assigned Kira to be a sort of handler for him. She talked to Brendan every day—pretending to be an alien.

His government sure was going the extra mile to help him recharge and get back on the job. He didn't want to admit how well it was working. If he knew he'd be working with Kira—that they might meet face-to-face—he'd ditch his lakeside cabin and head back to civilization in a heartbeat.

He wasn't sure when it had happened or how, but their talks had become the highlight of his day. He thought about her all the time. He even dreamed about her. Maybe today was the day he would tell her how he felt. After Paige's brush with death, he didn't want to risk never telling Kira the truth. Even if it made him feel like an idiot.

Falling for his handler was bad enough, but somehow he'd convinced himself that she felt the same way about him. He was probably going to make a royal fool of himself.

He flipped off his transmission, watching the power draw levels drop. Waiting—but never for long. He adjusted his headset and leaned forward.

"Brendan Sloan." Kira's voice flowed into his ears, rich and deep and sexy as hell.

He closed his eyes and smiled before responding. "Kira I'm-too-mysterious-for-a-last-name."

A hint of laughter laced her words when she spoke again. "I thought today's broadcast was going to be about your theories on the best spots in the Sol system for setting up extra-terrestrial bases."

"I changed my mind."

"That's a shame. I'm looking to build a summer home."

He let out a laugh. Talking to Kira always made him feel…less alone in the universe.

"For you, only the best," he said. "Earth all the way."

"No bias there?"

"Come on. Try to stop and smell the roses on Jupiter, and you get a chest-full of ammonia crystals."

He was encouraged when she let out a little snort, so he continued.

"Then there's Mars," he said, "with its barely-there atmosphere and all those satellites taking pictures. How's anyone supposed to have any privacy? And robots running around on the surface, poking and prodding everything. I wouldn't want to live there."

"Right. Because once robots move in, there goes the neighborhood."

"They're up all hours whirring and running around. They pretend they're collecting samples, but you know they're just partying."

She laughed and it about did him in. He wanted to see the face that belonged to that steel-and-brandy voice. He could imagine her sitting across from him on the couch, leaning her elbow on the back of the cushions as they talked long into the night.

"Besides, you don't need to build a summer house in the Sol system—you're welcome in my cabin any time. There's no guest room, but it has a big bed."

He cringed the moment the words left his lips. *Smooth.*

Still, his mind leapt at the chance to add him to the scenario in a very carnal way. He shifted in his seat.

"And a very comfortable couch," he said. "Which is where I would be…in that event."

"It's a tempting offer, but I'm kind of stuck here."

"Right."

Wherever *here* happened to be. Probably a bunker outside of Bethesda.

He imagined her working in a sort of call center for handlers—everyone with headphones on, sitting in their cubicles and listening to their assigned assets while they shot rubber-bands at homemade dartboards.

"You sounded a little tense," she said.

"Picked up on that, did you?" Of course she did. Nothing seemed to slip past her notice.

"Do you want to talk about it?"

He shook his head, even though he knew she couldn't see him. "Just had a close call. Too close for comfort. It's made me think about not taking things for granted. Or letting opportunities pass."

She was silent, so he went on.

"Look, I know you're my handler."

"I have said no such thing."

"Right. I forgot. You're an alien." Because *that* was more likely.

"I've never confirmed that, either."

"Yeah, and you haven't denied it. When you first

responded to my transmission, you wouldn't tell me how you picked it up and the only people capable of doing that are the ones in the group I work with."

"Or the advanced alien civilization you're trying to reach."

"There you go teasing me again."

"Sorry."

He could practically hear the smile in her words. It was contagious.

"I may just be a nerd to you—"

"You're not *just* anything to me," she said.

There was heat to her words. That was much worse than teasing him about being an alien. If she didn't care, why would she get so worked up? Why would she say something like that? He expected her to backpedal, but her tone was still serious when she went on.

"I wasn't supposed to talk to you," she said. "I'm just here to listen. But I couldn't...*not* respond. I had to talk to you, to get to know you. And I don't regret it. No matter what happens next, I'll never regret getting to know you."

His heart picked up. It sounded like she was saying goodbye.

"What's going on?"

"There have been some changes here," she said. "Big changes. I don't know when it will happen, but it's only a matter of time before I'm removed." Her voice cracked and she coughed as if she was clearing her throat.

His stomach felt like it had suddenly turned to lead. No daily talks with Kira to look forward to? No one to bounce ridiculous ideas off of and philosophize about society's ills and strengths?

The loneliness that had plagued him throughout his life started pushing back into his heart. He knew she had been lonely too, before they started talking. He could hear it in her voice. It was part of what bound them together. In all the world—in all the universe—they had found each other. He didn't want to lose her.

"I'm shocked they haven't already shut me down," she said.

His dread increased.

If she was anything like Eric, she'd been trained as a spy —received the full package. Brendan never let himself consider the baggage associated with being a handler. Sure, he considered that she might be using techniques to win his heart and seduce him into a course of action that might not be his own choice, like going back to work early. But hearing her talk about being *shut down* brought other aspects of her role to light. Ugly possibilities.

"Are you safe?"

"Yeah, just in deep trouble. But I don't care." Her voice was strong—almost harsh. But it softened as she went on. "Talking to you, getting to know you…has been the greatest experience of my life. I wouldn't trade it for anything."

"If your job was to convince me to come back, it worked. Tell them it worked. Tell them whatever they need to—"

"Hang on a second."

There was a pause when all he heard was the blood rushing through his ears.

"Something's wrong," she said. "I have to go."

"Kira, wait," he said. "I love you."

The signal died.

Chapter Two

"I love you."

Kira was already shutting down their com-link as Brendan said the words. She sat stunned, staring at Earth through the main planetary viewport of listening station T5-Alpha.

He loved her?

When he'd started talking about pair-bonding in his transmission, she couldn't resist the urge to imagine herself in that role with him. But it was a dream. There was no way they could be together—not after she'd broken Coalition protocol by making unauthorized contact. Her future was an eight-by-eight cell—if she was lucky.

A normal soldier would get a mind-wipe and return to duty. Kira was not normal. She couldn't let anyone find out how very not-normal she was.

Her performance levels were low enough that the genetic engineers who created her considered her a glitch. Thankfully, they decided she was salvageable as long as she was augmented with a nanNet. She couldn't be wiped unless they removed the network of nanites from her brain first, and if they tried...

Her stomach cramped. If they found out how very wrong she had turned out, they would want to figure out where they made their mistakes. By any means necessary. She had a feeling a cell would be paradise in comparison.

Thinking about it was too much. She needed to focus.

She activated the control-band built into the forearm of her uniform. Her biodata displayed, showing everything within normal parameters. An image of her face rotated in the upper-right corner.

The geneticists had selected brown hair, brown eyes, and skin that looked tanned even though she hadn't been in direct sunlight...ever. It was really too bad that her levels were so low. At least she *looked* like the Sadirian ambassador they had hoped she would become.

Shaking her head, she dismissed the screen and pointed the station's scanners at the patch of clouds that held her attention. The vid-screen in the band gave her a magnified view.

There it was again—light reflecting off something metal. Something rising out of the planet's atmosphere.

General Serath had departed on the *Arbiter*—the lead vessel in the Coalition's fleet—only hours ago. There were no Coalition-approved spaceships on the planet. The vessel approaching—and she was sure it was approaching—wasn't following protocol.

Not that anything about this assignment had followed

protocol.

The *Arbiter* hadn't even checked in with her while it was in orbit. If it hadn't been for the monthly contact with the planetary liaison, she would think she had been forgotten. Observers normally were only assigned a planet for six months. She'd been listening to Earth for two years.

After finding Brendan, she wasn't eager to be reassigned. That was why she had waited for the *Arbiter* to contact her. When the *Arbiter* left orbit, she was confused but relieved. At least she would have a chance to tell Brendan goodbye. Glancing back at the approaching sliver of light, she wondered if that "goodbye" would be more permanent than she originally anticipated.

"T5-Alpha, I need an ID on the vessel currently approaching the station."

After a brief delay, the station's interface sounded through the communications output of her control-band, level and emotionless.

"No vessels are on approach."

"What?" Kira looked back out the viewport that followed the curve of the small, disc-shaped station. The ship would reach them in minutes. It wasn't even cloaked.

Wait, the station *was* cloaked. How did they even know where she was?

For a moment, she considered that it was a coincidence. An unknown ship was departing from Earth and just happened to be on a direct collision course for the invisible station.

Unlikely.

"I have visual contact. Scan again."

The delay was a bit longer, but the interface came back with, "No vessels detected."

Something had to be wrong with the scanners, but she didn't have time to run a full diagnostic check. If the station wasn't detecting a threat, it wouldn't defend itself—or her. Not without her help.

The approaching ship was close enough that she could make out its shape—a small equilateral triangle getting bigger by the moment. Adrenaline spiked through her system.

"It's the *Tau Ceti!*" Kira jumped to her feet and ran toward command, hunching over to stay clear of the low ceilings while shouting orders to the interface. "Raise shields. Send a distress call to the *Arbiter*."

"Shields inactive. Communications are offline." The station made the statements casually, as if it wasn't reciting their death sentences.

"By whose order?"

"Access code 471-PLT-113894—planetary liaison. Earth designation Todd Simms."

Kira's fingers were slick with perspiration as she climbed the ladder that led to the upper deck. Coincidence was no longer a possibility.

The *Arbiter's* communications with the Coalition had

been logged with the station while it was in orbit. She knew that the planetary liaison had been taken into custody. What she didn't know was why his codes hadn't been stripped or who was using them.

The command deck was the most open and spacious part of the station, with a lowered circular area surrounded by monitors facing its center. One person standing in the middle of the circle could see everything, commanding the station as necessary. Kira ran to the center of the space. A chill swept through her as she looked around.

One by one, the monitors flickered out. The station lights dimmed and she heard systems shutting down all around her.

She was too late.

Her heart pounded as she walked to the viewport that made up one wall of command. The Tau Ceti ship approached at a steady pace, as if they knew her dilemma. They had probably caused it.

Listening stations weren't built to withstand attacks. Nobody cared about the data she gathered and analyzed except anthropologists and bureaucrats. Her reports probably never made it past the planetary liaison's desk.

The liaison...who had been taken onto the *Arbiter* right before it sped out of the Sol system. The man who had secured her assignment, convinced her that there wasn't an oversight when the months turned into years. The one who insisted that her reports go through him instead of directly to the Coalition.

He had come onboard the listening station three times since she'd arrived, to "check in and make sure she was holding up okay". The last time, he had insisted on doing a systems check.

She ran to the nearest console and keyed in every command she could think of, trying to get a response. Nothing. He must have put in a failsafe—programmed a code that would give the Tau Ceti control even if his standard codes were stripped.

She closed her eyes and took a deep breath through her nose, then blew it out.

Any moment, the Tau Ceti would open fire and destroy the station. They might not even know she was onboard. Except if they were working with the liaison, he would have told them. Wouldn't he?

With the access they obviously had, if they wanted her dead, they could vent the station or open the airlocks. Her uniform would keep her alive for a few hours, if they didn't vaporize her.

Life support was still on but the lights were dimmed. Dim lighting would help the Tau Ceti, protecting their sensitive eyes. They must be planning to board the station. What could they want, though? All she had was data, and the liaison could easily have shared all of her reports with them.

Except for the most recent one. They must be looking

for something.

Whatever they wanted, she had to stop them from getting it. If she could get to the sun-facing side of the station before they docked, she had a better chance of... What? Taking out as many of them as she could? Hiding for a few extra minutes before they found her?

If it came to that, she would end her own life. The first thing the Tau Ceti did after hatching was cannibalize the rest of their broodmates. They called it their own twist on genetic engineering. "Only the strongest survive."

They applied the same principle throughout their lives—not just at birth. The strong survived by eating the weak, even if the meal consisted of sentients. The thought turned her stomach.

She wasn't bloodthirsty by nature, but she had been trained as a soldier. Strategies formed in her mind as the ship loomed closer. She was running out of time.

Countdown. She smiled as the idea popped into her head. She might even survive.

She wasn't just a soldier. She was augmented.

She wasn't just a glitch. She was an aberration.

The liaison knew about the nanites in her brain that enhanced her memory and provided her with a direct link to download her interpretations of what she observed. The nanites made her singularly qualified to be assigned to a listening station. He had probably shared that information with the Tau Ceti. Which meant they knew that she had a constant backup of the station's data in her head—including the data they were after.

But she was a glitch. Glitches started their lives surprising the geneticists who tried to control their DNA. The engineers who had augmented her would be shocked to know the nanites were more than just an upgrade to her brain. They were her constant companions. Her friends.

The station might not defend her, but her nanites would.

She took a deep breath and held it. This was going to hurt.

Her awareness of them started as a tingling at the base of her skull. It rapidly moved through her brain till it concentrated on her forehead. The station's systems were locked out to her, but the nanites had a way with machines that she didn't. She willed them to make the connection.

Searing pain tore through her mind as the nanites powered up and sent their broadcast. Her brain felt hot, her skull practically cooking the skin under her hair. She groaned as she fell forward, hands planted on the console before her. The monitor flickered.

Her command was simple—self-destruct.

In ten minutes, the station would explode in a fiery burst of energy. The cloak generator was in the most protected part of the station so that it would be the last to go. Even if someone happened to be looking in her direction, by the time light could escape the field, the Earthlings would only see a bright flare that quickly winked out. Coalition destruct sequences didn't leave anything behind except an energy signature.

Because her nanites could convince the station that they were part of its systems, there wouldn't be any notifications or broadcasts. All she had to do to survive was drag herself to the escape capsules and hope that the chaos of the explosion covered her departure—or that all the Tau Ceti were on board when it happened.

She gave the nanites a few moments to reorganize themselves within her brain, then sent a shut-down command to let them rest. They weren't intended for that kind of use, and she imagined it taxed them about as much as it did her.

Swallowing was hard. Her mouth was bone-dry. Walking was worse. But she focused on putting one foot in front of the other, wincing as the pain in her head retreated to a dull throbbing ache.

She reached the escape capsule just as she heard the docking clamps engage. The airlocks were a level above. She was in the underbelly of the station.

Heavy footsteps sounded above her, the quiet station suddenly filled with echoing shouts and guttural yells. She waited as long as she dared, hoping to give more of the Tau Ceti time to board the station. She wanted as many to be caught in the explosion as possible. If she was really lucky, their ship would be disabled as well.

The voices were getting closer. She slid into the capsule

and programmed the first coordinates that came to her bruised mind. As the capsule detached from the station, she let out a deep sigh and closed her eyes.

Chapter Three

Brendan sat at his table in front of a plate of cold bean burritos. He only vaguely remembered preparing them. Going through the motions of making lunch calmed him down enough to know that he wasn't going to have an appetite for a while.

His first thought had been to call Eric, but he wasn't sure that was the best idea. If this was a ruse to get Brendan back on the project, that would be playing right into their hands. If it wasn't...

Two ideas presented themselves. Either Kira really wasn't supposed to talk to him, and letting Eric know about it would possibly get her into serious trouble, or she was in such serious trouble that Brendan might already be too late to help her.

He pushed away from the table and started to pace. The cabin was too small. Stifling him. He couldn't think.

He walked outside and slammed the door behind him. A walk along the lake's shore would help clear his head.

Two courses of action. Call Eric or don't call Eric. Maybe he could make the call, but sort of hedge around the issue. Maybe he could ask Eric to talk off the record. Of all the people Brendan had worked with, Eric was the only one Brendan trusted. It was still a lot to ask.

His chest ached. He rubbed it absently, staring out over the water. He wanted to hear Kira's voice again.

Summer had settled over the mountains, but the air kept a hint of the crisp snap of snow nearby. Sunlight glinted off the lake, reflecting the peaks in the distance and the pines that lined the shore. A cool breeze made the trees sway and reminded him that he probably should be wearing a jacket over his long-sleeved shirt.

It was peaceful—until something rocketed past him so fast that its slipstream nearly pulled him off his feet.

He stumbled forward, arms flailing as he regained his balance. The projectile was about the size of a car, only shaped like a bullet. It was hard to make out details, since the whole thing was chrome, gleaming in the sun.

His mind tried to make sense of what he was seeing. Some kind of low-flying plane? A missile?

That last possibility made his stomach clench. Maybe Kira wasn't the only one in line to be shut down.

If it was a missile aimed for him, though, they had missed. The thing was speeding away.

Halfway across the lake, it slowed to a stop and... hovered above the water.

Brendan rubbed his eyes and looked again. It was far away, but he could swear it was at least four feet above the surface, ripples spreading beneath it. It turned back in his direction and approached slowly.

"What the hell?"

His instinct told him to run and his curiosity told him to move forward. He settled on staying put.

The object stopped when it was only a few feet away, definitely hovering above the water. Its exterior looked like chrome, but it was shaped more like a quartz crystal than a bullet.

Six planes made up its body, the sides about ten feet in length with four-foot wide and three-foot tall pyramids formed on both ends. It swiveled around him, keeping the apex of one pyramid pointed at his chest. Then it drifted down to rest on the water.

After a few moments, the top panel of the object popped up, revealing a compartment within. The panel slid to the side, folding seamlessly into what he could now tell was some sort of aircraft.

Or spacecraft.

Brendan shook his head. No way. It couldn't be. He took a step closer and stood on his tiptoes, trying to peer inside.

Something moved and he jumped back. A figure rose from the opening, clad in shining silver fabric that clung to her form like a second skin.

At least, he thought it was a *her.* He couldn't be sure, because she was wearing a helmet that looked like it was made from the same opaque gleaming metal as the capsule.

Whoever—or whatever—was inside the suit had a gorgeous figure. Long legs, curvy hips, narrow waist, and a chest graced with two—and only two—breasts.

Brendan held up his left hand in the Vulcan salute and said, *"Klaatu barada nikto."*

The figure stood motionless for a few more moments, then lifted a hand to her helmet. She tapped the side and parallel lines appeared in the smooth chrome as it broke into one-inch segments. The segments folded back on each other until the woman's head was uncovered.

Well, uncovered by metal.

The breeze lifted her long strands of chestnut hair, obscuring his view at first. She shook her head to get her hair out of her face, and time seemed to slow like in a swimsuit commercial.

Dark eyebrows curved gracefully over her large brown eyes. Even as far away as he was, Brendan could see how thick and long her lashes were. Her nose was straight and narrow, her cheekbones defined, her chin strong, and her lips full and sensual.

"Brendan Sloan." Her voice was steel and brandy. The same voice he'd heard every day for months.

His stomach was in his throat, his chest tight enough he could barely breathe. He was so lightheaded he thought he might pass out.

What a first impression that would make. He managed to get hold of himself, forcing air into his lungs so he could breathe her name.

"Kira…"

She brushed the last unruly strands of hair behind one ear and smiled. The way her cheeks pulled up, the crinkles around her eyes, the dimples…

Kira was here. She was safe.

And standing in a spaceship.

He had made so many jokes about her being an alien. He thought she was playing along when she danced around the issue rather than calling him out on it. But now—

That sexy as hell voice of hers pulled him back to the moment as she said, "I come in peace."

Chapter Four

Kira couldn't believe that Brendan stood right in front of her. He was even more beautiful than she'd imagined.

He stared at her with blue eyes—wide and expressive. The sunlight shimmered on his pale skin. His red hair was short, sticking up in disheveled spikes on top of his head, then settling down to frame his face in a neatly formed beard that covered his jaw and chin. The beard drew her attention to his full lips.

She had only seen beards on people in the data she screened from Earth's broadcasts. The genetic engineers seemed to do their best to minimize body and facial hair on Sadirians—except for eyebrows and eyelashes. Well, and the pubis. They generally stayed away from that area.

She loved Brendan's beard. She wanted to run her fingers along his jaw and feel its texture.

The thought shocked her. Why would she want to do something like that?

Shaking herself, she focused on her immediate problem —the danger they were both in. If the Coalition found her talking to an Earthling, Brendan would get a mind-wipe and she'd end up in prison. If any Tau Ceti survived and managed to track her down, she and Brendan were just plain dead.

When she had put in Brendan's coordinates, she hadn't been thinking clearly. She was still putting her brain back together after the minor miracle she'd pulled off with the station.

Looking at him now, being so close to him, she couldn't honestly say that she wouldn't have come anyway.

She'd wanted to meet him.

Now she needed to keep him safe. The only way to do that was to keep the Coalition and the Tau Ceti from finding them. She needed to be off their scans, which meant no tech. Her nanites were already powered down and she planned to keep them that way for now.

She unlatched the bands at her forearms that held her uniform's controls, then did the same to the collar that held the segments of her helmet. With that out of the way, she grabbed her uniform's seal and slid it open down the length of her torso.

"Whoa," Brendan said. "Um, Kira?"

She glanced at him, noting that his eyebrows had hiked way up his forehead. A quick look at their surroundings didn't reveal any threats. The escape capsule should notify her of predators as well. For the next few minutes, anyway.

"What is it?"

He stammered for a few moments, then asked, "What

are you doing?"

"Stripping." She wiggled out of her uniform till it was around her ankles, then unlatched her boots and stepped out of them.

"I can see that. I can really, really see that." He shifted his weight and clasped his hands in front of his body. "But why are you doing it?"

"Coalition tech shows up like a nova on scans. My uniform and the escape capsule are filled with it."

She grabbed the capsule's med-kit and tossed it to Brendan. He scrambled to catch the small metal case.

"The med-kit is shielded from scans, plus its tech is inactive."

She keyed in the destruct sequence—manually, thank the stars—then programmed new coordinates that would take the capsule deep into the lake before it exploded. She sat on the edge of the capsule and swung her legs over the edge before sliding into the shallow water.

"Wait!" Brendan dropped the med-kit and rushed forward, water splashing up his jeans.

Gravity was faster.

As the water closed around her legs and waist, the cold hit her like a blow. Her knees gave out and she sank deeper before Brendan grabbed her and lifted her from the lake. One arm was under her knees and the other around her back. Her arms settled around his neck without needing her command.

After a few gasping breaths, she managed to say, "Much...colder...than...expected."

"This lake is fed from runoff from the mountains." Brendan gestured with his head across the water to snow-capped peaks.

That explained why her skin was covered in bumps and her heart was trying to beat its way out of her ribcage both as punishment and to escape from the stinging cold. Kira had been through a lot in her training, but liquid water wasn't all that common. And cold water was very different from the freezing atmospheres her teachers had exposed her to—in her uniform.

The option of taking it off while stranded on an alien planet hadn't been covered. It was generally believed that if things were bad enough to take out their uniform, the soldier wearing it would be dead anyway.

But she was alive. And she intended to stay that way.

The orientation session that prepared her for her assignment in Earth's listening station gave her rudimentary knowledge of the environment and things she might encounter if she had to go planetside. It was a rarity, and she certainly had never heard of it happening under the circumstances she was facing.

She pulled on her training anyway, trying to calm her heartbeat. Deep slow breaths, focus on the objective. But all she could seem to think about was Brendan's warm chest pressed against her side.

The escape capsule silently drifted away from them, then sank under the water when it was several meters away.

"Where's that going?" Brendan asked.

"Under the water so the explosion won't be visible."

"*Explosion?*"

"The water should protect us from the blast."

"That's not particularly reassuring." Brendan was already headed for the shore. It didn't take long for them to clear the water.

He bent so she could grab the med-kit. As he stood again, he said, "How far away do we need to—"

A dull boom-whoosh sounded behind them. Brendan flinched, tucking Kira closer against his body, wrapping more of his around her.

He was protecting her.

The thought made the bumps on her skin intensify. Held in his arms, she had the same internal sensations as she did in zero gravity.

He looked over his shoulder at the spout of water that was already starting to fall back to the lake. "Okay. I guess that was that."

"I would have told you if we were in danger."

"Right. Because showing up in an escape capsule that you then promptly destroy is a sign that everything's peachy keen."

"Peachy what?"

"It's an idiom."

He stared into her eyes for long enough that she grew uncomfortable. Her stomach was fluttering and her skin still tingled from the cold. Strangely, she felt hot at the same time. Especially where they touched. The feeling spread to…places she was not used to paying attention to.

The form-fitting undergarments she wore under her uniform were wet from the lake water. She was cold and her body was trying to find equilibrium. That was all it was.

She knew the thought was a lie.

"You're shivering."

His voice was gravely and lower than usual. His pupils were dilated too, as if he was excited.

It was probably from the shock of her arrival—not from her proximity. She wondered what her nanites could tell her about what else was going on in his body.

"Clothing would be useful given the cool temperature in the region," she said.

Slowly, he let her go, as if he didn't want to. The ground shifted beneath her feet. Sand. It squished up between her toes, abrading her skin.

She was about to say something when Brendan pulled his shirt up and over his head. Sunlight gleamed along his shoulders and highlighted the smooth skin of his pectoral muscles, abdomen, navel…

Something deep inside her destructed as her gaze seemed locked at the fastener for his jeans. Heat pooled in her belly, tingling spread between her legs. She felt almost like she'd taken a hit of *Coupling*, only the effects were much more intense.

"Here."

He handed her the shirt. It was still warm from his body.

"Won't you be cold now?"

"My cabin isn't far. I'll live."

She handed him the med-kit, then slipped into his shirt. The soft fabric whispered across her skin. A rich, sweet scent surrounded her. Brendan's scent.

He took her hand and started to lead her toward the grass. Earthlings referred to *blades* of grass. But he wouldn't lead her into something dangerous. She trusted him.

She stepped onto the green foliage.

The plants poked at her skin, tickling the sides of her feet. She took another step. Both feet were on the life-forms. The leaves were cool. Some of the sand stuck to her was wiped away. More of it seemed to be grinding deeper.

Cygnus X, she was a soldier. She had been trained to withstand torture. But she had never been planetside before. Not in an undeveloped, pristine environment, teeming with life.

She paused and said, "Wait."

"What's wrong?" Brendan turned to face her, creases appearing between his eyebrows.

Focusing on him made her feel better. She gripped his

hand more tightly.

"There's too much... Too many..." She shook her head and closed her eyes. Even that wasn't enough to shut out all of the stimulae.

Birds were singing nearby. The hush of processed air whispering through the station's vents had been replaced with leaves rustling in the trees. The swells and ebbs of the wind were nothing like the steady drone she was used to. They left her breathless, made her wonder what would happen next.

She opened her eyes and looked up at the sky—a clear and crystalline blue with a few fluffy white clouds breaking up the monochromatic backdrop. Very different from the speckled black canvas visible from the station's viewports —from every viewport she had ever used.

The wind picked up and the trees bent, branches turning over and leaves waving like thousands of tiny hands. It was beautiful and terrifying.

"I don't think I can walk," she said.

"Are you hurt?" He stepped closer, but not close enough. She wanted to wrap her arms around him and hold on forever. Or at least until they could get inside.

"I'm not hurt. I'm just...overwhelmed. I've never been outside of... Well, I've never been outside before."

"You can't be serious. Don't you have...planets where you're from?"

"We do, but they're mostly dome-worlds or otherwise

covered in tech. I was raised on space stations and ships. I've only been planetside for training." Training that seemed absolutely inadequate at the moment. "And there was no grass. And I had shoes."

Planets like Earth were rare. They were valuable. That was why the Coalition had assigned Earth preservation status. Most soldiers were unlikely to ever encounter a planet so rich in life. Her training hadn't covered anything like the springy green plant-matter beneath her feet.

"Are you agoraphobic?" he asked.

"No, there's just…so much here. Clouds and birds and —" She swatted at a small flying insect that buzzed past her face.

"I get it." He smiled. "Earth's a happening place. I tried to tell you it's the only place to be in the Sol system."

She surprised herself by being able to smile back at him. "I came for the company, not the scenery."

That…was not what she meant to say. It was the truth, though. She cleared her throat and looked away, but not before she caught how the furrows between his brows eased.

"Come on." He let go of her hand and turned around, then crouched in front of her.

"What are you doing?"

"I'm going to give you a piggyback ride."

"A what?"

"Lean forward and wrap your arms around my neck.

Just don't choke me."

He shifted so that his back was brushing her stomach. Was this some sort of Earth mating ritual? She shook the thought away.

He patted his shoulder, as if encouraging her. She leaned into him, holding onto his neck carefully.

"I'll need you to carry this." He handed her the med-kit, then said, "We're playing hot potato with this thing."

"Hot potato?"

"Forget it." He laughed, then reached back and gripped her thighs. She let out a gasp as he lifted her into the air, with most of her weight spread over his back.

"Relax." His voice was gentle. "I've got you."

The fluttering in her stomach intensified as he started walking, carrying her along with him. She felt like she'd been given too much *Balance*—the chemical mixture most Coalition citizens used to maintain their contented state of mind.

She hadn't used it herself for years, though the Coalition made sure she always had some on hand. Even the med-kit had several vials. But she hadn't bothered with *Balance* since she'd been sent on her first assignment.

Balance always gave her a weird buzz that she didn't like. Maybe it was because she was a glitch. She was more likely to use *Coupling*. The physical release it generated was enough to keep her content. Too bad *Coupling* wasn't part of a standard med-kit. She could introduce Brendan to

Coalition mating rituals.

Moons, where had *that* thought come from? She glanced at Brendan, but looked away quickly. Her face was probably as red as a skeelbat's belly.

At his age, Brendan was statistically likely to have had multiple sexual encounters—none of them involving a drug that would take care of everything for him. Earthlings did things manually.

Kira was suddenly very aware of his hands on the bare skin of her legs, on her chest and pelvis pressed against his back. His hands were large and strong. And warm. All of him was warm. She wondered what it would be like to snuggle up with him under a blanket and explore their anatomical compatibilities.

"You okay?" he asked.

She had never lied to him and wasn't about to start. "I'm not sure. This is weird."

"*You* think this is weird? I'm the one giving a piggyback ride to an alien."

She laughed and started to feel a bit lighter. She had made it this far. The Coalition would send someone to investigate what had happened to the listening station. She would be presumed dead, if they even knew she had been there in the first place. They would discover the Tau Ceti involvement when they scanned the energy field of the explosion and take action. She wouldn't have to do anything.

And she could live out the rest of her days happily on Earth. Once she acclimated.

"You not wanting to be found…" Brendan said. "Does it have anything to do with you talking to me? You said you weren't supposed to make contact."

"That's part of it. My superiors wouldn't be happy to find out we've been communicating. But they aren't the ones I'm worried about."

"Okay, now *I'm* a little worried."

"Don't be. All my tech is destroyed or offline. As long as we don't fire anything up, they shouldn't be able to find me."

"But doesn't that mean you're stuck here?"

"'Stuck' isn't the word I would use."

A stream of words came to mind. Giddy, happy, relieved.

Free.

A small structure came into view nestled in the trees that lined the lake. Its walls were wood and the roof was hidden under an array of primitive solar panels. Antithetical to the space stations and domes where she had always lived, and yet…comforting.

She let out a sigh and relaxed against him. A feeling similar to safety washed over her. Similar, but stronger. She couldn't put a word on the emotion until Brendan did it for her. He opened the door and stepped inside.

"Home sweet home."

Chapter Five

Brendan felt Kira slide down his back with every nerve-ending in his body. He didn't want to let her go—to stop touching her—and now he was losing his excuse.

With all the questions about who she really was and where she was from rattling around in his brain, only one kept repeating itself.

Had she heard him when he told her he loved her?

That led to more questions. Did her people even have love?

He hoped so. His heart clenched at the thought of her not being able to reciprocate his feelings.

"Thank you for helping me," she said.

He realized he was staring at her. Had been for a while.

"Sure. Of course." He shook his head and closed the door. "I'm sorry. This is a lot to absorb, you know?"

"I can imagine." She looked around the small room, curiosity lighting her features. "This is your home?"

"One of them." He wished she was seeing one of his bigger houses. Then again, after being raised on space stations and ships, maybe she'd be more comfortable in the cozier space.

The cabin had a great-room design and was built for practicality above all else. In front of them, an octagonal wood-burning stove provided a means of cooking food as well as warmth for the right half of the room. The kitchen took up the corner on the far right from the door, his desk and all his equipment filled the other right-side corner. A free-standing counter in the center of the space sort of separated it from the rest of the cabin.

He had put his couch as close to the stove as he dared, which wasn't as close as he would like. He also didn't like that it meant he would be sitting with his back to the door, but he didn't use the couch that much anyway. A fireplace set into the middle of the left wall supplemented the heat, and when he built it up, the stones would warm and hold enough heat to get him through most nights. It also helped to heat the bathroom, which was behind a door in the far left corner.

His bed was to their left. He tried really hard not to think of the bed.

"What's that smell?" she asked.

Brendan sniffed the air. All he detected was wood smoke. Well, that and his burritos.

She walked to the counter and stared at them, practically salivating.

"That's my lunch. Are you hungry? I can make you something fresh."

"No thanks. I mean, yeah, I'm hungry, but don't go to any trouble."

"It's no trouble at all. But if you want those, go ahead. I wasn't going to eat them anyway."

She gave him a brief smile, then put her med-kit on the counter. She picked up a burrito and sniffed it, then took a bite. Her eyes rolled shut. He watched her eat another few bites, reacting as if it was the most delicious thing she'd ever tasted.

"I'm guessing you don't have burritos where you're from," he said.

"*Burritos.* No. This is delicious." She licked some refried beans from her thumb.

"Cold bean burritos. There's not even any cheese in there. What is it that you normally eat?"

"Nutrient bricks. They have everything we need in a compact package."

"Sounds like soylent green."

"What's soylent green?"

"People."

Her eyes widened and she paused mid-chew. Then she spit her food back on her plate and started wiping at her tongue.

"Relax! Relax, it was a joke. That's not made of people."

She gave him the clearest *what the hell?* look he'd ever seen. He did his best not to laugh.

She cleared her throat, then asked, "Is there a place I can get this sand off my feet?"

"Yeah. The bathroom is right through there." He pointed to the bathroom door. "I can show you how the shower works."

"Thanks, but I think I can figure it out."

"Okay. Well, *H* is for hot water, not that there's much of it. I'll find you some dry clothes."

After she disappeared through the door, Brendan ran his hands over his face again, then just held them there. How could this be real? How could any of this be real?

Kira in his home. An alien. He didn't know which was harder for him to believe.

He heard the water start to run in the bathroom. Yeah, she was here all right. Whatever else he believed, he was sure she needed his help. He kicked himself into gear.

Fires were already burning in the fireplace and stove. He grabbed a few extra logs from the firewood rack and built up both heat sources as quick as he could.

He had just kicked off his boots when Kira emerged from the bathroom. Her eyes were wide and she held a roll of toilet paper in one hand and paper towels in the other. Nightmare scenarios played through his head. He should have made sure she understood how toilets worked.

Brendan didn't mind roughing it, but he infinitely preferred working facilities. He had no idea how Kira would adjust if she had destroyed their only toilet by filling the pipes with paper towels.

"My training covered this," she said, holding up the toilet paper.

Thank God. He let out the breath he'd been holding in a little puff.

She held up the roll of paper towels, her jaw set and a determined look on her face. Her voice shook a little when she spoke, though.

"But what in the name of the Solar Cross is *this* for?"

It took him a moment for his mind to recover. There was no disaster in the bathroom after all. And her expression... She was obviously trying not to freak out, and seeing both items right next to each other, he couldn't blame her. The thoughts that must be going through her mind.

Brendan laughed, hard. "That's for something else entirely."

She arched an eyebrow. "Care to elaborate?"

"Those are paper towels. They're for cleaning up spills and drying stuff. Like, you could use them to dry your feet, for instance. I keep a roll in the bathroom for when I get behind on laundry and don't have any clean towels. Just throw them away in the little trash can in there when you're done."

Kira stared at the paper towels for a few moments longer, as if she was deciding whether or not she believed him. Finally, she said, "Okay." Then she turned and walked back to the bathroom.

Brendan was still chuckling as he peeled off his jeans and put them on the drying rack near the stove, along with his socks. Kira should probably put her clothes on it too.

The thought of her naked was more powerful than the cold, and his boxer-briefs started to tent. He grabbed the quilt from the back of the couch and wrapped it around himself. Which was good, because when Kira emerged from the bathroom a moment later, she was completely naked.

Her long legs were bare, her hips curving and then dipping gracefully into her narrow waist. The curves just got better the farther up his eyes travelled, rounding her small but perfectly formed breasts and stalling at the dusky skin of her nipples.

Brendan dropped his eyes to keep himself from staring at her breasts, but then they latched on to the dark curls between her legs. He bounced his gaze up to her navel and suppressed a groan.

Her stomach was perfect. Flat abs faintly outlined under the smoothness of her lightly tanned skin, a gentle line flowing up from her belly-button...

And he was staring at her breasts again.

"These clothes are wet," she said. There was nothing suggestive in her tone, but that voice of hers... She crossed the room to the drying rack and draped the shirt he had given her and her undergarments next to his jeans. He hadn't even noticed her carrying them.

He snapped his gaze to hers when she turned back to him, doing everything in his power to maintain eye-contact. He bit his lips and pulled the quilt more tightly around his shoulders.

"Did you find clothes for me?"

"Hmm? Oh right." Brendan was grateful both for the distraction and that Kira would soon be clothed. "There are drawers built into the bed."

She nodded, then turned and crossed the room. Dear lord, that ass... He let out a little grunt.

Looking back over her shoulder, she asked, "You okay?"

"Yeah, I'm fine. Absolutely... Things are great." He looked up at the ceiling, then down along the walls.

Brendan had never been that great with women. Being a ginger nerd had not helped. Once he'd made his first million, interactions became even more difficult. It seemed like everyone he met would feign interest to try to get close to him, then eventually realized you couldn't fake geek. When he sold his company at just the right moment and that *m* turned to a *b*, he had all but given up on forming a genuine connection with anyone.

Kira was bringing him back to his nerdy high school days, designing robots in advanced engineering classes and exploring computer systems he really shouldn't have been getting into.

She knelt and opened a drawer. Rooting around, she stood with one of his long-sleeved shirts. She draped it over her head, lifting her arms through the sleeves as it settled around her body. He didn't know he could be jealous of a piece of clothing, but in that moment, he sort of wanted to be that shirt.

She bent over, nearly killing him as the hem rode up to just below the curve of her ass. His shirts were long, but she was tall. His brain calculated their heights and he realized that if she braced herself on the bed, they'd be perfectly aligned for…

This was not helping. His dick was so hard it hurt. He made sure the quilt was covering him, keeping his arms out from his body enough that he hoped she wouldn't notice.

"I can grab some clothes for you too." She rifled through his shirts.

If he tried to get dressed in front of her, she'd see how worked up he was. Even grabbing the shirt from her was out of the question. He didn't want to let go of the quilt for a moment.

"I'm good."

She glanced back at him, one dark eyebrow raised high on her forehead. Then she shrugged and stood. She pushed the drawer shut with her foot before walking back to him.

"There's another quilt on the couch," Brendan said. "I recommend wrapping up and sitting near the wood stove."

Maybe he should sit far from it. Cooling off could help. He thought about running back to the lake and diving in.

She ran her hand over the quilt, looking up at him with a

shy smile. "You don't mind?"

"Of course not. What kind of host would I be if I let you freeze?"

Half a dozen sci-fi movies hit him at once that made his off-handed comment send a chill through him—stories where aliens used human bodies as hosts. He shook off the thought, but was grateful for its calming effect on his body.

His dick was already starting to calm as she wrapped herself in the quilt. He let out a sigh of relief when she was covered.

"You sure you're okay?" she asked.

"Yeah."

They walked around opposite sides of the couch and sat facing each other. The warmth from the wood stove washed over him, helping to banish the last of the chill from the lake water. He stared at her for a moment of comfortable silence.

Kira. The woman he'd talked to every day for months. That he'd laughed with, teased, offered his heart to…

She kept her head bowed a bit as she smiled at him—a shy smile, but gorgeous. Then she laughed and leaned back against the couch. His heart gave a little jerk in response. Warmth spread through his chest that had nothing to do with the quilt or the fireplace or seeing all of her incredible body and everything to do with knowing she was safe.

Chapter Six

"I can't believe you're actually here."

Kira laughed, her stomach fluttering. "That makes two of us. I suppose you'll want answers to those questions now."

"Only one matters at the moment. Are you okay?"

Of all the questions to start with... Her throat felt tight. She coughed so she could answer him.

"Yeah. I have a bit of a headache, but trust me, it was much worse for them."

"Them who?"

Right. He would need context. Kira wasn't used to talking to other people.

"The station was being boarded by hostiles. I set it to self-destruct."

His eyes went wide and his mouth dropped open. She stared at his lips again. They looked soft.

"Kira."

He scooted closer, then picked her hand up from her lap. He held it in his, tracing his thumb over the backs of her fingers.

More bumps spread over her skin. Tingling spread through her chest and down her belly, pooling between her legs. It reminded her of *Coupling*, but felt so much better. She could feel her nipples brushing against the shirt she had borrowed from him.

She swallowed hard.

"Are you all right?" he asked again, emphasizing each word.

"I... No."

That wasn't right. Of course she was fine. She was alive, uninjured, and had secured a safe location to regroup.

"What happened?"

She shook her head. "You can't tell anyone any of this. You know that, don't you?"

"I kind of figured. Don't worry, I won't tell anyone about you. And I won't let anything happen to you."

It was such a sweet sentiment. But if the Tau Ceti or even her own people showed up, Brendan wouldn't be able to stop them. Neither would she.

He waited patiently. Ready to listen to *her*. That was new. She was in this far, and he deserved the truth. She trusted him with it.

"I am an alien," she said.

His lips tightened a bit. She noticed because she was still staring at them. She couldn't seem to look away.

"I'm part of a Coalition of planets that has—well, had— a listening station in orbit, watching Earth's broadcasts and observing your development. It was automatically gathering data and compiling it, then sending it to a committee for review until about two years ago when I was assigned to the station. I was told to start parsing the data before it was sent, which is usually a sign that a planet is nearing a tipping point."

"What kind of tipping point?"

"There are a variety. Maybe the planet was getting to a point where they were ready for first contact. Or a big event was imminent—like a war or a meteor impact—and the committee wanted someone there to get the best record possible."

"That's not reassuring."

Neither was the truth that she had pieced together. "Don't worry. I'm pretty sure in Earth's case it was something else."

"I'd worry less if you were smiling."

She smirked and shook her head. "It's a simple story of corruption."

"Again, not really helping me relax."

She took a deep breath and tried to explain everything again. "Earth is designated as a nature preserve. You have no idea how rich this planet is in resources or how rare that is. And the planetary liaison assigned to manage Earth was just arrested. I'm certain that's not a coincidence."

"That doesn't sound good."

"The head ship of the fleet—the *Arbiter*—was involved.

I'm sure everything will be sorted out in short order. Except for me. I think the liaison used his connections to have me assigned to the station so that he could filter the reports I was sending to the Coalition. When the *Arbiter* left orbit, no one contacted me. I don't think they know I'm here."

"My equipment can send a signal. You can let them know—"

"I don't want them to. I don't want to be found. I want to stay here...with you."

"Oh..." He looked puzzled, but then his face relaxed and he smiled. "Oh."

"I mean, I can figure something else out. But after all our talks, I thought—"

Brendan didn't let her finish her sentence. He released her hand so that he could cradle her face, pulling her close as he leaned toward her. Those soft lips gently brushed against hers.

Stars...

Kira melted into him. That was how it felt. His lips moved on hers slowly, gently coaxing her response.

She had used *Coupling* with other people a few times. It had always seemed more mess than it was worth. Kissing had not been involved. If it had, she might have formed a different opinion.

Rising on her knees, she kissed him back. His lips were warm and strong. They parted to let his tongue slide along her mouth. When she gasped, he pushed his tongue deeper.

She moaned against his mouth, opening herself to him, pressing her chest against his body. Her tongue tangled with his as she gripped his shoulders and pushed him back against the couch. At some point, she had shifted to straddle him and his hands had moved to her hips. She wasn't even sure when, but she loved it. She loved feeling his firm grip, the heat of his kiss, the hardness of his...

Moons, his...member...was poking her belly. Without the aid of *Coupling*.

Of course he could hold an erection without the Coalition drug. Earth mating practices were far different from what she had experienced. Giving and receiving pleasure from another person using only their bodies... Kira wanted to know what that was like. With Brendan. Immediately.

Contact, stimulation—touch and friction.

Clenching her fingers on his shoulders, she slid up his body. He hissed in a breath and moved his hands to her ass. She felt muscles deep within her responding.

The cotton of his boxer-briefs was so thin. She rubbed herself along his length, groaning as the tingling between her legs grew into a current of electric pleasure coursing through her. Nothing had ever felt so good. Not *Balance*, not *Coupling*. She wanted more.

He tilted his head to the side, breaking their kiss. That just gave her a better angle to reach his neck. She latched onto his skin, layering kisses and nips as she worked her way up to his ear.

"This is all happening kind of fast," he said. "Not that I'm complaining. But are you sure you want—"

"Yes." Stars, she was sure.

Reaching between them, she slid her hand down the hard plane of his stomach, tracing the ridges of his abs. She didn't stop until she hit the elastic of his waistband, stretching it so she could reach him.

"I've heard this called a cock," she said, wrapping her fingers around him.

He groaned and his eyes rolled shut. "Um, yeah. That's one word for it."

She applied more pressure, watching his response. Loving it. He leaned his head back against the couch, eyes still clenched shut, lips tight. He pulled in deep draws of air between long pauses, as if all of his body's attention was on her hand.

Stimulus. Simulation.

He groaned as she started moving her hand on him, mimicking mating. She imagined what he would feel like inside of her, filling her. More electricity arced through her body, this time centering from between her legs, even though he wasn't touching her there.

How could her body be doing this without *Coupling*? Without even being touched?

If they had used the drug, they would have already climaxed by now. She wondered what else they could do in the time their bodies needed to respond naturally to each other.

"In one of the broadcasts I reviewed, a man who swore he had encountered aliens called them *cocksuckers,* as if it was a bad thing." It didn't make sense. The heat and wetness of her mouth would be an even better simulation than her hand. "Is that a bad thing?"

She watched his throat move as he swallowed.

"That's a loaded question."

"I want to give you pleasure."

He gripped her wrist and pulled her hand away from him.

"What's wrong?" she asked.

"You don't have to do this." His expression was grave. "I'll help you no matter what."

"I don't understand."

"You don't have to trade sexual favors to get me to help you."

She felt her eyes grow wide. "People *do* that? Seriously?"

"Well… Yeah." He shrugged, scowling at her.

Kira started to laugh. She couldn't help it. The idea of trading sex for anything was so…*alien* to her. That thought made her laugh even harder.

"Care to clue me in?" Brendan asked.

"I'm sorry. That's just one of the funniest things I've ever heard."

She wiped at her eyes as she sat back so that her weight was on his lap. He picked up the quilt that she had cast off and threw it around her shoulders, keeping his scowl in place. She had a feeling it was mostly for show.

"People in the Coalition... Well, they don't really have sex," she said. "Not like on Earth, anyway."

"See, now you're just making me uncomfortable." He grinned a little, letting her know he was joking. But she could sense there was a thread of honesty woven into his statement.

"There's a drug called *Coupling* that we can use instead of having sex. It takes care of everything."

"Your people only have sex alone?"

"Not always. For some, it doesn't satisfy all their needs. Those people pair up and use it together."

"Nobody just...gets it on the old-fashioned way?"

"Gets what on?"

"Has sex."

"Oh. Not that I've ever heard. And I'm a very good listener."

She loved talking to Brendan, but she wanted to do other things. It had been too long since he had kissed her. There was too much space between them. The energy that had been building in her was threatening to turn to frustration. She wanted to go back to pleasure.

She leaned forward and brushed her nose along his neck, then pressed a kiss there. He didn't relax into her as she'd hoped, so she pulled back again.

"What is it?" she asked.

"You've done that before, though. Right?"

"Done what before?"

"'Coupled' with someone. Used that stuff with another person. I mean, you're not…"

"I've had sex before, if that's what you're asking."

He let out a breath. "Okay. Cool. Because this is going fast and it's already complicated enough and—"

She kissed him again, pressing her lips to his firmly to make sure he received the message. She wanted this—wanted him—for no other reason than that he was himself.

Chapter Seven

For someone from a culture that didn't exactly have actual sex, Kira sure knew how to kiss. And the way she had gripped him… Every touch, every look was equal parts naivety and confidence. He didn't know how she pulled that off. His dick didn't care—it just wanted more.

He was glad his boxer-briefs were still in place. Otherwise, he'd have been tempted to just slide into her. As compatible as their bodies seemed, he wanted to make sure they took precautions.

Gripping her ass to hold her, he leaned forward, then stood. Their quilts fell away as she held onto his shoulders and wrapped her legs around his waist.

"What are you doing?" she asked.

"Taking you to the bed." He started across the room.

"Oh. Okay." She gave him another of those megawatt smiles. He had to pause for a moment to kiss her properly.

Kira in his arms. He didn't care if she was an alien or not. She was the person who knew him best in the universe. The person he loved.

He broke off the kiss and carried her to the bed, setting

her down on the side closest to his bedside table. The fire he had built up chased the chill from the air, but he left her shirt on to keep her warm. There was still plenty he could do and reach.

Kneeling before her, he ran his hands up her calves then under her thighs. Her lips parted and she hissed in a breath.

"When you take that drug, do you touch each other?" he asked.

"Not like this." She shook her head, her smile faltering. "It's more like a lot of awkward hugging. That's how it always felt to me, anyway."

"That doesn't sound very appealing."

"I only tried a couple of times. I don't think—" She cut herself off, eyes widening as if she had caught herself before letting a secret slip through.

There was no point for him to try to keep his secrets from her. The technology she had demonstrated already left his *advances* centuries in the dust. No wonder she'd been able to pick up his signal—she was the intended audience.

He hoped eventually she wouldn't feel the need to keep things from him either. He wanted her to trust him fully, like he trusted her.

"You can tell me anything," he said. "I thought you knew that by now. Especially with everything you've already shared."

She pinched her lips together so tight they disappeared. But she nodded.

"I'm not…normal."

"Oh." Maybe their anatomy wasn't as compatible as he thought. "If there are things I need to know before we go further, tell me. I can handle it. I just… I want to be close to you."

"I want that too."

She put her hands on either side of his face and kissed him again, then rested her forehead against his for a moment. When she leaned back, she had that determined look on her face that he had seen while she was programming her escape capsule to detonate.

"Coalition citizens are genetically engineered," she said. "Part of that is being designed so drugs like *Coupling* work well with our physiology."

"That's profoundly disturbing."

She let out a snort. "What's disturbing is that they don't work on me the way they're supposed to. *Coupling* is okay if I use it by myself. But *Balance* just makes me feel… weird."

"Balance?"

"It helps us maintain emotional equilibrium."

"Your government drugs you to keep you happy?"

This was the worst foreplay ever. But Kira's desire to stay on Earth made a lot more sense.

"There are septillions of people in the Coalition. *Balance* helps keep the peace. The species that can't use it are invariably the ones who initiate conflict."

His stomach started to twist. The aliens he'd thought might take him to a more peaceful society were real. And he wanted nothing to do with them or their version of peace.

Well, most of them. Kira was an exception.

"Peace at that price—" he said.

"I shouldn't have brought it up."

She leaned away, frowning, then shook her head.

"How do you do it?" she asked.

"Do what?"

"Manage all of these emotions and still function? How do you have sex when there's so much conflict? So many thoughts competing for your attention?"

"You're right. This isn't the best topic during sex."

They had plenty of time to talk later. She looked lost. He wanted to help her feel safe and at home, both in his cabin and in her own body.

"We do it by listening," he said.

That caught her attention. After being on a listening station, he thought it might make the most sense.

He ran his hands along the outside of her thighs. "We listen to what our bodies tell us."

Her smile returned—the shy yet confident look he loved.

"I am a good listener," she said.

"Then let me change the topic to something more central to our current interests."

He slid his hands under her shirt, massaging her hips.

She took in a deep breath, then let it out slowly.

"That's really nice," she said.

"I'm glad to hear it. What about this?" He brushed the backs of his fingers along her stomach and she jumped, then laughed.

"That tickles."

"Good to know."

He increased the pressure of his fingers, gripping her sides and running his hands up along her ribs till they were just below her breasts. Her smile faded and her eyes drifted shut as he cupped her breasts and gently massaged them.

"Um... I don't..."

"Do you not like it?"

"Oh no. I like it."

He ran his thumbs over her nipples. She gasped and her eyes flicked open.

Brendan smiled at her. "Do you like that too?"

She nodded. "Quite a bit."

He rose on his knees and slid his arms behind her back to pull her closer. She bent down and kissed him, running her tongue across his lips. He opened his mouth to her, meeting her thrusts with his tongue, relishing the feel of her, the taste.

Trailing his lips down along her neck, he spent a little time there before moving farther down. He nuzzled her breasts through her shirt and she gasped. He grinned, then closed his mouth over her nipple. He ran his tongue around it, flicking it through the fabric. She let out a moan. Nuzzling her chest, he moved to her other breast to do the same.

"Brendan, I feel…"

He paused and shifted back, intending to ask her if something was wrong, but she grabbed his face again and kissed him. Her tongue delved into his mouth and she scooted closer to him. When she let him go, they were both panting.

"I feel…need," she said.

He leaned forward, cupping her sex with one hand. Her eyes went wide and her mouth dropped open. He pressed his fingers against the wetness at her core, swirling them around her clitoris.

"Moons! What are you…? That's…"

"That's me talking to your body with mine."

"Yes." She braced herself on her arms, leaning back and letting her eyes close again.

Cautiously, he slid a finger deep into her. Her breath hitched. He circled her clit with his thumb, slowly moving his hand. When he thought she was ready, he added another.

"Oh… That's…"

"Only a beginning," he said.

She opened her eyes, bright with curiosity. He smiled at her, then leaned forward.

Chapter Eight

Kira's body hummed with pleasure. Her arms tingled, her legs burned, and an ache was building between her legs that she didn't quite understand. She wanted to throw herself on Brendan, to slide her body against his until she found how they most perfectly fit together.

He had other ideas.

His fingers were moving inside her. She wouldn't have believed how good it would feel if someone told her people could do this sort of thing. And the external stimulation was even better.

He shifted his thumb aside and leaned forward. She felt her body tense at the uncertainty of not knowing what he would do next, but reminded herself that she trusted him. She trusted him like she'd never trusted anyone before. So when he bowed his head to her, she didn't pull away.

The first kiss was...remarkable. The tingling she had been experiencing seemed intense to her until the shockwave of his lips on her clitoris rippled out through her, exponentially increasing her pleasure.

Her arms trembled, but she forced herself to stay

upright. She wanted to see what he was doing to her, to learn as much as she could.

Her skin was heating, almost like when she used her nanites in unorthodox ways, except there was no pain. Only pleasure. It built as his tongue made quick flicks and slow circles over her clitoris. His fingers kept moving within her, sliding in and out, over and over and—

Something deep within her broke loose. Like a dam that had been holding her back from fully experiencing her body. It vaporized in the heat of the thrumming ecstasy that tore through her.

Her head snapped back as she cried out. Still, he kept going. The stimulus threatened to overwhelm her. How much pleasure could one body take?

And yet, part of her wanted more. She wanted him inside of her, to join their bodies the way *nature* intended rather than the Coalition.

"Brendan," she gasped. She was practically panting.

He didn't pause, but looked up at her. Another wave of pleasure wracked her body. At this rate, she was going to pass out.

Or climax again.

His lips became gentler, pulling on her clitoris as he slid a third finger deep into her core. There was no build the second time. The climax hit her in every cell simultaneously. Her blood was alive, her molecules radiating energy. Everything was light and fire.

Moons, she wanted to wrap her legs around his neck and pull him closer.

"Enough!"

He finally stopped, leaning back at her outburst.

She was going to push him to the ground and jump on top of him. But he was still wearing his boxer-briefs.

"Take those off."

He smiled and said, "Yes, ma'am."

She pulled her shirt over her head and threw it away as he complied. The air was cold to her heated skin, so she pulled back the covers and crawled to the center of the bed. When she turned back around, Brendan was standing next to the bed completely naked.

Cygnus X, that cock...

Her mouth went dry and she licked her lips. After what he'd done to her—for her—ideas cascaded through her mind of how she might reciprocate. Even those thoughts made her core clench, surprising her. If thinking about it could cause such a response, what would it be like to actually take him in her mouth?

"I can guess what you're thinking, but I wouldn't last thirty seconds right now," he said. "We have plenty of time."

He opened a drawer in the table next to his bed and pulled out a shining square packet. For a moment, dread shot through her. Did Earthlings use something like *Coupling* after all?

The change from the near-euphoria of the pleasure he had given her made her dizzy. She took a deep breath and let it out slowly to steady her nerves.

He opened the packet and pulled out a small circle of flexible material. As she watched, increasingly fascinated, he held his gorgeous cock in one hand, then put the circle on his tip. He unrolled the material over himself till his cock was covered in a transparent sheath.

"What's that?"

"A condom. It helps prevent pregnancy and the spread of disease. We seem pretty compatible, so I figured it would be a good idea."

"That's a very good idea." And one that would never have occurred to her otherwise.

When she was assigned to observe Earth, her system had been prepared to handle the native pathogens, but she had never given any thought to preventing pregnancy. *Coupling* took care of birth control for both parties. But now that she was thinking about it...

Moons, she could get pregnant. She could carry another life within her body.

"Are you okay?" Brendan asked. "You look like you're about to hyperventilate."

"I'll be fine. Those things work, though, right?"

"Nothing is foolproof, but I've trusted them so far. If this is too much for you, we can stop."

"I don't want to stop," she said.

She wanted more. And even if his systems weren't one-hundred percent effective… The thought of a life she made with Brendan did a lot to ease her fears. She wouldn't be in it alone.

She had a feeling she would never really be alone again after this.

"Kiss me?"

He smiled and crawled toward her on the bed. "Gladly."

Then his lips were on hers and he was pressing her back against the sheets. Bliss.

He pulled the covers over them as his body covered hers. The hair on his thighs prickled against her legs as he nestled between them. She felt his cock resting just outside her core, waiting, ready to enter her.

Lifting himself up on his elbows, he brushed her hair away from her face. "Are you sure about this?"

"Absolutely."

"Thank God," he murmured, as he pressed himself deep.

The experience was revelatory.

Without the drug, she felt every millimeter of contact, even with how quickly it happened. She felt her body expand, her muscles contract around him. Her nerve-endings were already on full alert after everything he had done, and her sheath was relaxed enough to welcome him.

When he was in as deep as he could get, there was no space between their bodies. His stomach pressed against hers, their chests touched so that their hearts rested against each other. He brushed his cheek against hers, then kissed her neck, giving her a moment of stillness, a moment to just *feel* everything.

It was almost more than she could bear. She managed to whisper, "I never knew anything could be like this."

He kissed her again, and there was so much tenderness and meaning in it. What had he said about handling the conflicting emotions? Listen to her body. She could sense that there was more waiting for them and she wanted to experience it.

He lifted himself on his elbows again as he started to move within her. The entire time, he held her gaze.

She gasped as he pulled himself almost from her, feeling a spike of anxiety at the thought that maybe he was ending their union already, but then he slid back in. She moaned as he filled her again. Nothing had ever felt so good or so right.

She wrapped her legs around his and rested her hands on his back, feeling his muscles flex with his movements. She explored him, letting her fingers trace the valley of his spine and the ridges of his shoulders, watching his expression, catching every hitch in his breath that let her know when she had reached a spot he particularly liked.

It was the very best kind of listening.

Her own body was uncoiling, relaxing with each thrust. At the same time, energy was building in her again. She could feel it pooling in her belly, radiating like starlight from where they were joined.

He closed his eyes and bit his lips, his pace increasing. She sensed the build within him, echoing her own. Running her hands down along his back till she could cup his ass, she focused on the feel of the strong muscles pulling him out, pushing him deep, faster and harder until a sonic boom sounded through her body.

It thrummed and vibrated, shaking loose every tense nerve, relaxing her on what must be a cellular level. She felt his cock pulse within her, echoing the throbbing of her muscles as her body held him within her, keeping him deep.

Brendan let out a huge sigh and lowered his head next to hers. He nuzzled her hair, then moved to her mouth for a lingering kiss.

She hoped it was the first of many more to come.

Chapter Nine

It was the end for him. Brendan was sure of it. He had found his "one and only" and she was from another planet.

The reality of it hit him as he took in the wonder on her face, as he felt the ease in his heart. He'd found what he had been looking for, but on his homeworld after all.

"That was incredible," she said.

"You aren't kidding." He felt his dick slide from her body and shifted his weight so he could lie next to her.

Kira rose on her elbow so that they were nose-to-nose. She grinned broadly. "Do you think we could do it again?"

Laughing, he said, "Are you trying to kill me?"

"What? Of course not. It can't really hurt you, can it?"

She was so distressed, but it only made him laugh harder. "I'm fine. I just need to rest for a little while. And then you can have your way with me all you want."

Her smile returned. "I like the sound of that. I had a few ideas…"

Time couldn't pass quickly enough. Damn biological limitations. He grabbed a tissue to clean himself up and tossed everything in the trashcan under the bedside table.

"Do you mind if I ask you some of my questions now? Might help us fill the time while we wait."

"Okay."

She pulled the pillow under her chin and wrapped her arms around it, lying on her stomach. Her body was putting off so much heat. He snuggled next to her, propping himself up on one elbow while he draped his other arm over her back.

"The most obvious one is, where are you from?"

"Sadr-4."

"Really? That's close."

"The galaxy is much more heavily populated than you might think."

"How come you're the only one who responded to my signal then?"

Her smile faded and she looked away. "Because I was intercepting it. That's part of my job. Well, *was* part of my job."

"That was going to be my next question. I want to know more about that listening station and what you were doing on it."

"Mostly screening broadcasts for evidence that Earthlings might be figuring out ways to prove that alien intelligence is real. The Coalition doesn't think that Earth is ready for that knowledge."

"Why do they get to decide?"

"Because they're the ones with the fleets of starships."

His stomach started to ache again. He did not like the idea of powerful aliens making decisions for his homeworld without even letting them know a question had been asked.

Was Earth ready? Okay, probably not. But the Coalition still should have asked...somebody.

"You're upset," she said.

"Disturbed is a better word for it. And disappointed. I thought aliens intelligent enough to be capable of interstellar travel would be a little more advanced when it came to politics."

He moved on to his next question, hoping to lighten the mood.

"How is it that we're so alike? You said your people are genetically engineered. Did they design you to fit in on Earth in case you had to interact with us?"

She laughed and shook her head. "No, everyone from Sadr-4 is like me—like you. Earth was populated by a colony ship that crashed here millennia ago. They took over from the evolving hominids, but lost touch with their history when their ship was destroyed."

What the hell? *He* was an alien?

"That's...going to take me a while to wrap my head around." He searched for another question while that knowledge sank in. "You say you're all genetically engineered, though. Why haven't you made more changes to...the design, for lack of a better word?"

She looked away, her mouth tightening into a line.

Way to flatter her, Brendan.

"I mean, you are amazing, but—"

She snorted and rolled her eyes. And not in a, "Oh, go on then," manner. She really didn't believe him.

"Seriously, you're the most beautiful woman I have ever seen."

"You don't have to say that." Her voice was angry and a little hurt.

"I mean it."

She glanced back at him, expression guarded, but a bit of hope seeping in. "We didn't change the design because it works for us. What's been changing is our technology and the level of control we have over the expression of our DNA."

"That explains why you're so—"

"Stop," she said, sitting up and pulling the quilt around her body tightly. "Just stop, okay?"

He sat up next to her, wondering what had offended her so badly. Maybe the Coalition had a different view of what was beautiful. He had seen something like that on an episode of *The Twilight Zone.*

"I'm sorry I upset you," he said. "But I won't take back what I said. I do think you're beautiful."

She let out a deep sigh and rested her head against her hand. "I'm not used to hearing that sort of thing."

"Maybe you should get used to it. Because I think

you're pretty great."

She let out a little laugh and shook her head. "I don't know how to take compliments. I've never been anything but average."

"If you're average, I don't want to see what passes for gorgeous among your people. My head might explode."

All that earned him was a tiny laugh. She closed her eyes and let out a soft sigh, leaning her head against his chest. He wrapped his arms around her.

After a long pause, she said, "It isn't just that I'm average."

He waited for her to continue. He could feel the tension in her body and didn't want to push.

"Sometimes the engineering goes wrong. The system glitches. That's what happened to me—what I am. A glitch."

She turned her head away. He shifted so that he could reach up and cup her chin, making them face again. Her eyes were glassy. It made him want to punch someone.

"You are not a glitch. You hear me? You're not a mistake."

A tear managed to escape her lashes and roll down her cheek. It was too much. He leaned forward and kissed her. He let the kiss build slowly, waiting till she relaxed—till she melted against him—to deepen it. He slid his tongue into her mouth, keeping his strokes gentle. When she pulled back, she sniffed and wiped her face dry.

"Thank you," she said.

"There's no need to thank me." What the hell kind of society did she come from?

"All of my test scores are average at best. That's why they installed a nanNet in me and assigned me to be an observer." She pressed herself against his chest. "I didn't really mind, though. I figured at least that way I could be useful."

"What's a nanNet?"

"It's a network of nanites that live in my brain. They help me store and parse through the data I collect."

"Hang on. They put a hard drive in your brain to make you more useful to society?"

Kira shrugged.

"That is so messed up," he said.

The irony of it killed him. She had done this so that she would feel more a part of her society, but from what he could see it had only served to isolate her.

"If someone's not born a rocket scientist or acrobat—that doesn't mean they have nothing to contribute," he said.

Kira was staring at him. He hoped he was getting through to her.

"We do things differently." Her voice was just above a whisper.

"Yeah. I see that. What about the voices of dissent?"

"Dissent?"

He took a deep breath and let it out slowly. With

everything she had told him—the drugs, the genetic engineering, making sure Earth didn't find out aliens existed—her society seemed all about control.

"Voices of dissent. The people who disagree. Who want to change society."

"There are no dissenters."

"There are *always* dissenters. How many people did you say are in the Coalition?"

"Septillions."

"And you think not one of them has a different idea of how things should be done?" When she didn't respond, Brendan went on. "Those are the voices you should be listening for."

Chapter Ten

"The only people I know of who oppose the Coalition are the Tau Ceti. And the last time I heard their voices, I blew up my listening station to avoid their interrogation tactics."

Kira didn't like much of what Brendan was saying. Primarily because it carried truth. But there was more going on than he was aware of.

"You have my complete attention," he said.

"The Tau Ceti joined the Coalition a few hundred years ago, which isn't long at all. It happened fast. Their homeworld is a swamp and has a peculiar electrical field that threw off our scanners. By the time we figured out that they were capable of extra-solar travel, it was too late to keep them pinned into their system."

"Why would the Coalition even want to do that?"

"Among other reasons, the Tau Ceti are cannibals."

"Oh. Yeah, I guess that's a good reason. No wonder my soylent green joke fell flat."

He was trying to ease the tension of the conversation, but she couldn't join him. She knew way too much about the Tau Ceti.

"Wait, they weren't going to…" His smile faded. "They wouldn't have—"

"They say they've stopped eating sentients, but there are still incidents. And after interrogating me, they would have needed some way to get rid of my body."

"Okay. Not liking the Tau Ceti. Why were they after you?"

"The only thing they could have been after is information. That's all the listening station had."

"Couldn't they have just grabbed it from the computers instead of interrogating you?"

"Possibly. My nanites were synched with the station, so they might have wanted to make sure all the data was destroyed. Whatever they were looking for, the only remaining copy is in my head."

"No wonder you don't want to be found. If tech is easier for them to find, won't your nanites be a problem?"

"Don't worry, they're powered down currently." Kira intended to keep them that way for as long as possible. "But you're right—even their tech signature would make me easier to locate with scans. I was able to grab the medkit because the tech inside is off. The only other contents are a few doses of *Balance*."

"That drug the Coalition uses to control people."

"They're not controlling citizens. It just helps people be happy."

"Tomato, tomah-toh."

"What?"

"Forget it." He shook his head again. "Why doesn't your super-friendly government use *Balance* on the Tau Ceti?"

"It doesn't work on them. Well, it works *too well*. The Tau Ceti started out as amphibian humanoids. *Balance* is applied topically. The Tau Ceti's skin somehow amplifies the chemicals and knocks them out."

"Good to know."

This would be a lot for anyone to absorb. He was handling it pretty well, so far. He shook his head, then leaned forward and kissed her. Slow, deep and wet.

When he pulled back, she asked, "What was that for?"

"You looked like you needed it. I know I sure did."

She smiled and leaned against his chest. He wrapped his arms around her shoulders.

"At least we don't have to worry about any space frogs running around on Earth," he said. "I imagine they'd really stand out in a crowd."

"Actually, one of the first things they did after joining the Coalition was to begin their own genetic engineering program to make them look more like us."

"I'm over here reaching for peace of mind, and you're just plucking it away."

"Sorry."

He was quiet for a long time. Then he asked the question she was dreading, that she hadn't even let herself think.

"Are they a threat to Earth?"

She didn't answer. He put his hands on her arms and shifted so he could look into her eyes.

"Kira, are they a threat?"

She couldn't lie to him. She wouldn't.

"I don't know."

"They want something on Earth," he said. "Otherwise, they wouldn't be here."

She wanted to argue the point, but anything she said would be grasping at straws. He was right.

"What's the Coalition doing to stop them?"

Another dreaded question.

"They don't know the Tau Ceti are involved."

He rose on his knees, pulling away from her.

"Yet," she said. "They don't know yet. I'm sure when they scan the debris field—"

"Kira, this is my planet we're talking about. My home. Everyone I love is here." He sighed and shook his head. "Do people in the Coalition even still do that? Love each other? Or is there a drug for that too?"

She understood where the hurt was coming from, but his words still stung.

"I'm sorry," he said. "I shouldn't have said that."

"I love you."

His gaze shot to hers. She smiled and reached for his hand.

"We still know how to do that at least," she said. "Love

each other. We call it pair-bonding. It isn't always about love, but we still feel the urge to partner with others."

"This is hard to process. I mean, we could be having a translation issue. That word could mean something different to—"

She wrapped her arms around his neck and kissed him, let her lips linger on his. Rising onto her knees, she deepened the kiss, shifted her hand to gently trace her fingertips across his cheek and down his chest.

She paused long enough to say, "There's no mistaking this. I love you."

Kissing him again, she let her body talk for her. She trailed her fingers down his chest, then pushed him back onto the bed. He rested his hands on her hips. She could feel his tension.

Of course he was distracted. There was so much going on, so many new things he was processing. She felt it too. But they would sort everything out. Probably sooner than she wanted.

They needed to know what the Tau Ceti were after—what information was important enough to get her listening station boarded. To sift through the data in her final report, she would have to turn on her nanites. The danger that would put them in would be deadly and immediate. And if their time together was going to be that limited, she wanted to explore everything she could first.

She slid down his body, kissing his chest and stomach

along the way. His cock had stiffened again. She wrapped her fingers around it and squeezed, simulating what her core had done earlier.

"Kira…"

She didn't want to start talking again. Not before experiencing this.

She wrapped her lips around him.

Brendan gasped. She lightened her grip with her hand while tightening her mouth, taking him in deeper. She could feel so many things. His heart pulsing through his shaft, his body tensing. She brushed her fingertips along his length, then down over his sac. His back arched. The change was subtle, but she felt it.

Movement, friction, pressure. Heat and wetness. She swirled her tongue around his crown before tightening her lips and sliding her mouth along his length. As she gently ran her nails over his sac, she increased her pace.

"Kira…"

His hips started to move—rising to meet her, synchronizing their movements. It was incredibly intimate, witnessing his reaction so closely. A thrumming pulse was building in him. She could feel it.

"Stop!"

He pulled her head away. Why had he stopped her? Was she doing something wrong?

"Condom," he said.

"What?"

He grabbed her arms and flipped her onto her back. For a moment, she thought he might just fall on top of her, but he held himself back. Instead, he scrambled for the drawer at their bedside and pulled out another of the metal packets. His hands were shaking.

She took it from him and smiled. He put his hands on his hips. His strong thighs were spread between her legs, his cock thrusting toward her. Maybe she'd never know what it was like to take him that way. But she'd had enough. And if this was their last chance to couple—to make love—she wanted to feel him inside her again.

She opened the wrapper, then placed the circle of transparent material on his crown. She rolled it down slowly, glancing at him as she did. He bit his lips. His control must be reaching a breaking point. When he was ready, she started to lie back, but he stopped her with a hand on her shoulder.

"No, this time it's all about you."

Chapter Eleven

Brendan dropped to his back, gripping one of Kira's thighs so he could pull her on top of him as he did. She was left straddling him, his dick resting against her slit. He wanted to thrust into her so bad he could hardly stand it. But if he did, he'd go off too fast, and she needed time to catch up.

She stared down at him with her eyes wide as if she didn't know what to do. He gripped her hips and started to move her, sliding his dick against her. She was a quick study and took over fast.

She rocked against him, swirling her hips. Even this was going to be too much if she kept that up. Lucky for him, she was more worked up than he realized. She shifted so that his dick was lined up, then lowered herself over him.

Bliss shot along every nerve-ending as she wrapped her tight quim around him. She took him in so deep—deeper than he thought she could manage. Her dark hair fell forward across her chest, brushing her breasts as she moved. She lifted herself up onto her knees, then slowly sank back down, over and over.

Brendan lifted his hands to her, brushing her hair behind her back, then lightly dusting his fingertips along the sides of her breasts. He flicked his thumbs over her nipples, letting his touch become firmer.

Her pace increased. She reached down to his hands and pulled them away from her so she could lace their fingers together. He followed her lead as she positioned his arms on the bed so that she could brace her weight on them, letting him support her. It opened them up to a new array of possibilities.

She leaned into him, making a swirling motion with her hips as she lifted herself up and then eased back down. The stroke plus the way her sex was clenching him was pushing him too close to the edge again. The pleasure was pulsing through his hips, gathering together steadily, his dick so full and ready he wasn't sure how he could last.

He thought about baseball, cold water, the stale bean burritos on the counter. Nothing helped.

Her pace increased, the frills left behind as she pumped him with her body, her hands gripping his so tight it almost hurt. He could feel her starting to pulse and let himself go, his hips rising up to meet her every time she crashed back onto him. She let out a loud cry as he felt her fall over the edge into her climax, her back arching and body pulling on him, urging him into his own.

The energy pooled in him flooded out as he came, his body spilling into her. His hips bucked and she rode him, thighs clenching him tight. His skin was on fire, a locus of energy radiating out from where they were joined.

She fell across his chest when the last waves of heat were settling in him. She made a soft contented sound as she let go of his hands. He wrapped his arms around her.

"I thought you said you came in peace," he said.

He felt her laugh as much as heard it, her body vibrating on his, humming with contentment and happiness. He wished they could stay that way forever. But he knew they couldn't. She must have felt the same.

"Kira…"

"I know." Her voice was quiet "I'm parsing the data."

"What, like now?"

"If we're lucky, the Tau Ceti are still recovering from the station exploding."

"And if we're not lucky?"

She lifted her head and kissed him. He could tell her attention wasn't entirely with him, though. He broke off the kiss and pushed them both up to a sitting position, shifting so that he could sit next to her.

"We can figure out another way. You don't have to—"

"I do. There is no other way."

He didn't know what to do, so he sat next to her and held her hand. Moments ticked by. They hadn't been vaporized, which he took as a good sign.

"I think I found something," she said.

"What?"

"A plane crash over Louisiana."

Brendan felt his stomach clench. "Yeah, I heard about that."

"Scans picked up an unusual reading. An energy burst. It wasn't long enough to run a full analysis. It could have been the Tau Ceti. But why would they take down a small passenger plane?"

"James Conroy was on that plane. He was a senator who just got elected. Is there anything in your data about him?"

"That name has come up several times. He was championing environmental issues."

"I thought you were just watching us to make sure we didn't realize aliens are real."

She shook her head. "No, my job was to make sure you didn't get proof."

Senator Conroy was all about stopping climate change. According to Paige, his first priority was convincing people that climate change was real and having a detrimental impact on Earth's ecosystems. Paige was helping him gather evidence for his reports.

"Why would an environmental activist show up in your reports at all?" It didn't make sense.

"Because of the geographical areas he was concerned with. The water sample reports the station accessed showed shifts in alkaline balance, temperature, and salinity that…"

He did not like the look on Kira's face. Her eyes snapped back into focus as her gaze met his.

"What is it?"

"They match the ecosystem on Tau Ceti-6. Their homeworld."

His heart started to pound. Aliens were real—okay. They were watching Earth. He could handle that, even them walking among Earthlings. But making permanent bases there?

"Are you saying that the Tau Ceti have changed Earth's environment to match their physiology?" He wanted to be crystal-clear on that point before he freaked out about it.

"I'm saying that they have destroyed indigenous ecosystems to make room for their own. This is worse than anything I've heard of them doing before. Raiding settlements is one thing, but this amounts to a full invasion of a preservation site. The sanctions they're risking…"

"Why would they do it? You said Earth is rich in resources, but what could they possibly be after? Gold? Gemstones?"

"The Coalition can mine asteroids. Minerals are abundant in the galaxy, and precious stones can be replicated in labs."

"What are we missing?"

"I don't know. I can't think of any reason the Tau Ceti would want to set up a permanent presence on Earth."

"They'd have to be found out eventually, right?"

"Maybe, maybe not. The Coalition is aware of the damage Earthlings are doing to their own environment. If the Tau Ceti keep their operation small enough and try to match the damage they're doing to what's already going on, they might be able to get away with it for decades."

"Shut down your nanites," he said.

She closed her eyes for a moment, then said, "Done."

The urgency he felt before at the thought of Earth being in danger coalesced into a chilling fear in his chest. Even if the Coalition figured out the Tau Ceti were involved in destroying the listening station, they had no idea what they were doing on Earth. And if the Tau Ceti managed to find Kira…

He shook his head, trying to avoid that thought. But he had to face it. If they removed her from the equation, who knew how long they could keep destroying Earth's ecosystems before the Coalition caught on.

He had no doubt his sister would fall in the line of fire eventually as well. Those water samples Kira mentioned didn't just hop into the lab on their own. Paige was Senator Conroy's main environmental scientist.

"Kira, we have to tell the Coalition what's going on."

She nodded. "I know."

Chapter Twelve

"Turning on my nanites will be nothing compared to this."

Kira watched as Brendan completed preparations to send his final broadcast. She had recorded a message that contained everything they had figured out about the Tau Ceti involvement on Earth. They would send the broadcast across a section of space that should ensure the *Arbiter* received it.

The transmission would need at least five minutes to complete and would show up loud and clear on any Tau Ceti scanners that were still functional. She was no longer just worried about the ship that had boarded the listening station. With an operation on Earth as big as they suspected, there were probably plenty of Tau Ceti waiting and watching for just such a signal. The question was whether they would be close enough to reach Brendan and Kira before they could run.

Brendan had resources. If they could reach civilization, their chances of survival would be better.

She wasn't holding out much hope.

"You ready?" Brendan asked.

She nodded, then rested her hand on his shoulder, leaning over him to watch him work. He put his hand on top of hers. They locked gazes for a moment, then he turned back to the controls and initiated the broadcast.

"There it goes."

"Are you sure they won't be able to recover any data?"

"I set up my equipment with a self-destruct. It won't take out the whole cabin, but there should be some pretty cool fireworks."

"You're kidding."

"What, you think you're the only ones advanced enough to have self-destruct buttons? Please. I worked for my government. I don't want this falling into anyone else's hands. You can't pull data from a system that's been both wiped and slagged."

"Too bad we can't time this one to take a few of them out."

The cabin was already precious to her. In only a few hours, she had built the best memories of her life there.

"Remind me never to make you mad."

She smiled, then leaned forward to wrap her arms around his shoulders and kiss his cheek. She nuzzled the soft hair of his beard. Stars, she hoped there would be time for more of that.

His smile suddenly vanished. "Part of it is an EMP. I was so distracted with everything going on, I forgot about your nanites."

"They'll be fine. They're powered down." She gave him another quick kiss. Her stomach was tightening as the broadcast neared completion. "You're not using nuclear fission for that, are you?"

Her sensors hadn't picked up anything like that near his cabin.

"There are other ways to create an EMP."

"Nothing that standard Earth-tech can make."

"Look around you. Any of this look like standard Earth-tech?"

He had a point. It was too bad Earth wasn't considered advanced enough to begin First Contact preparations. Brendan would be a perfect candidate for the preliminary committee.

His computer beeped.

"That's that." He shut down the broadcast, then keyed in the commands for the self-destruct. "We have ten minutes to make ourselves scarce. My jeep is about a five minute hike if we hustle. The EMP won't reach that far. I know you say you'll be fine, but I'd just as soon get you far from here before it goes off."

"Let's go, then."

Brendan headed for the door while Kira ran to the counter to grab the med-kit. Sunlight spread across the floor briefly, then was blocked. The hair on the back of her neck stood on end.

"Um, Kira?"

She turned around, knowing what she would see. Brendan had his hands in the air and was backing toward her. Two Tau Ceti entered the cabin.

The Tau Ceti had done their best to look like Sadirians, but there were imperfections in their process. Their mouths were too wide, faces too tall and long. And their eyes, while within Earth norms, were much smaller than Sadirians'.

One was a foot soldier, fully decked with cybernetic enhancements. As if that wasn't enough, he was carrying a laser rifle in his muscular arms. The other was tall and lanky, wearing an Earth-style business suit. His skin was pale and he had dark black hair. Somehow, the awkwardness of his features lent him an eerie sort of handsomeness. He hadn't bothered with a weapon and didn't look augmented like the other.

"Well, this is quaint." The leader's voice was low and smooth.

His soldier closed the door behind them, then took up a guarding stance.

"It isn't much, but it's home," Brendan said. "Welcome, Mister…?"

"St. John. But you can call me Horatio."

"Horatio? Okay, then. I'm Brendan. This is—"

"K-58-b7. Born during cycle 12 on Sadr-4 station 9 to batch 31. It wasn't a very good batch, I'm afraid. Full of glitches. Kira. I'm well aware."

"I'll thank you to show some manners while you're in my house," Brendan said. "Kira's not a glitch."

Brendan glanced at Kira. She shook her head tersely, but it wasn't enough to stop him from reaching for her hand. She didn't take it. It didn't make a difference. Horatio noticed.

"Uck, this compulsion you Sadirians feel to pair-bond is bizarre. It makes you vulnerable. Lucky me." His smile was nothing less than sinister. "You did a very good job concealing yourself, my dear. Didn't spare yourself so much as a laser cutter. I bet you're wishing you had a little something now, aren't you? Coalition tech can be addictive for your kind. It's a shame, really."

He walked over to Brendan's equipment, looking everything over.

Stars, don't let him notice the destruct sequence.

"Pretty sweet setup, eh?" Brendan said. Maybe he was thinking the same thing, trying to distract the Tau Ceti. "Best Earth has to offer."

"I don't know. I'm rather fond of those little robotic vacuums Earthlings have developed. But I suppose this was able to get the job done, so to speak."

"I can show you how it works," Brendan said.

No way. That would get him way too close to the equipment. Then again, maybe that was the idea. Try to take the Tau Ceti out with the self-destruct somehow? Maybe Brendan was thinking about that EMP too.

Disabling the foot soldier's cybernetics would help even out their fighting abilities.

"I'm not concerned with how it works, but rather what it was used for. The transmission was encrypted with a Coalition code we're not familiar with." Horatio turned back to them. "Let's get to business. You're both going to die. The question is how unpleasant the experience will be and who will go first. The best thing you can do is cooperate."

Even if the EMP took down the soldier's cybernetics, she wasn't sure she could take both of them. If only she had a weapon. Kira's skin was tingling with the urge to do something.

Wait, skin...

The med-kit had several doses of *Balance*. If she could splash them with it, they would be incapacitated.

She reached for Brendan's hand and squeezed it to let him know she had a plan. She only hoped it would work.

Chapter Thirteen

Horatio Cannibal Space-Frog had stepped a bit away from Brendan's equipment. He was still close enough that he was about to get a nasty surprise. By Brendan's count, the EMP and fireworks should happen any minute.

The problem was, Kira was still in the cabin. At ground zero. She was confident having her nanites powered down would protect her, but Brendan wasn't so sure. He held her hand tighter.

There was nothing they could do about that. But maybe they could learn more while they waited for the big boom.

"So…from what Kira tells me, you guys are risking a lot being here on Earth. What is it—the scenic views? Bean burritos?"

Horatio snorted. "Something like that."

Brendan looked over at Kira. "What is it with you aliens and bean burritos?"

"You know, if we're going to die anyway, I want to finish that one," Kira said. She tugged his hand and led him to the counter.

"Whatever makes you happy," Horatio said. Which was

weird. "Stay on this side, if you please. I do need to keep you where I can see you."

Kira hopped up onto the counter and patted the space next to her. She was up to something. Brendan only hoped it was enough to get them out of this.

Horatio and his bodyguard didn't seem to mind. Kira picked up the bean burrito and took a bite, staring at their unwelcome visitors as she chewed.

"You don't seem very worried about the signal we just sent," Brendan said.

Horatio shrugged. "The *Arbiter* left orbit yesterday and is well on its way to Sadr-4. It'll take it at least a day to return. That gives us some wiggle room. The Sadirian wants a last meal. What about you? What would make you happy?"

"I want to know what you're up to on my homeworld." Brendan figured he might as well go for it, since the guy asked.

"I don't see the harm."

Seriously? This guy was going to spill his master plan? Had he never seen a James Bond movie?

Horatio smiled as he walked around the cabin, looking at the fireplaces and feeling the fabric of the quilts. "We're really not so bad. All we want is to make people happy."

"Why?" Brendan asked. "There's always an angle. What's in it for you?"

"Naturally occurring oxytocin, primarily. With a few

other yummy human feel-good hormones thrown in the mix."

"Oxytocin," Brendan said. He looked over at Kira.

"It's the main component in *Balance*," she said.

"But you Tau Ceti guys can't use *Balance*."

"Ah, very good," Horatio said. "I see you've been learning about us already. Yes, synthetic *Balance* doesn't react well with our physiology. It's much too concentrated to be truly enjoyed. But a similar mix of chemicals in the wild…"

"Wait…" Kira set down her burrito. "You're harvesting oxytocin from humans?"

"We find it has a much smoother finish and a better buzz." He looked at Brendan and said, "You needn't worry too much about your fellows. We have a strict catch and release policy. After we feed, the human is returned to the wild. Our geneticists have worked up some modifications with the latest generation. We don't even need tools for harvesting."

Horatio leaned his head back and opened his mouth wide, revealing a pair of sharp canine teeth hanging down from the roof of his mouth. Brendan put his arm in front of Kira and leaned to the side so he was partly blocking her. Not that it would do a lick of good against that nasty looking weapon the heavy by the door held.

Horatio laughed. "You know, pair-bonding makes the blood much sweeter, the hit more…stimulating."

"Vampire space frogs," Brendan said. "You guys are freaking vampire space frogs? You have to be kidding me." Horatio laughed. "That's a rather apt description, I suppose. Although we've left most of our frogishness behind."

"It wasn't an improvement, from what I can see," Brendan said.

"What? All our humans are free-range," Horatio said. "It makes the chemicals more pure when we harvest them. It's too bad we can't keep you two alive. I bet you'll be tasty. But we can't run the risk of you escaping when there's a whole planet of humans we can feed from. Which brings us back to your final usefulness. I will ask only once, and then I will start removing appendages. The Sadirian knows this is not an empty threat. What was in that broadcast?"

Brendan's computer beeped. Thirty seconds.

"What was that?" Horatio asked.

Brendan shrugged. "Primitive tech. It's noisy."

He and Kira grabbed for each other at the same time, swinging themselves over the counter and onto the floor. She reached out and snagged the med-kit on the way.

His equipment let out a final beep, then he heard a crackle-bang as the explosives detonated. Sparks flew over their heads and Brendan smelled the acrid scent of burning electronics.

If all went according to plan, the EMP would have gone off at the same time. The space frog by the door had metal devices obviously worked into his body, making him a *cyborg* vampire space frog. More fodder for the nightmares Brendan hoped he survived to endure. The grunts he heard from the direction of the door encouraged him, as did the fact that Kira seemed unfazed.

She opened the med-kit and pulled out two clear vials. She popped the lids from each and handed one to Brendan.

"*Balance,*" she said. "Don't get it on your skin."

Brendan nodded. He wasn't sure what she had in mind, but followed her lead as she jumped up from behind the counter. The cyborg space frog by the door was bent double, his arms dangling heavily from his shoulders. Brendan thought maybe that was it for the guy, but he straightened and took a few jerky steps toward them.

Kira flung her vial of *Balance.* The liquid splashed onto his skin and within seconds a blissful expression covered his face. He sank to the ground, eyes closed.

"Where's the other one?" Brendan asked.

Kira slammed into him, knocking him clear as something dropped from the ceiling, landing right where he'd been. He turned and saw Horatio crouched on the floor in a stance no human could achieve. Well, not without several broken limbs.

"How many knees and elbows do you have?" Brendan asked.

Horatio grinned, then leapt at Kira.

"Look out!" Brendan shouted. His warning was

unnecessary.

She dodged to the side, spinning around and landing a brutal kick into Horatio's ribs. Brendan had never seen anyone move so fast. The force of the impact propelled Horatio into the wall of the cabin. Instead of bouncing off and hitting the floor, he sort of...stuck there. He looked at Brendan with eyes that blinked sideways.

"That's just wrong," Brendan said.

Horatio launched himself at Brendan, his fangs gleaming in his wide-open mouth. Just before he reached Brendan, Kira brought both her arms down on his back, fists clenched together in a hammer of flesh and bone. This time, Horatio hit the floor.

Kira lashed out with another kick, catching Horatio under his armpit. He made a screeching noise, then collapsed. She nudged him with her foot. She was barely panting.

"That was so hot," Brendan said.

Kira raised an eyebrow at him and he shrugged.

"I'm just saying." He finally remembered the vial in his hand and flicked some of the liquid on Horatio. "Take that, vampire space frog."

When he looked back at Kira, she smiled.

Chapter Fourteen

Kira tucked herself deeper into Brendan's side as they snuggled in front of the fire. He had wrapped them both up in a quilt after making her a cup of tea. Her bare feet were pulled up next to her on the couch, and she was more comfortable than she had ever been.

The door to the cabin burst open. She and Brendan looked over their shoulders at the two Sadirians that leapt into the room. They were dressed as Earthlings, which was a bit of a surprise. Their arrival wasn't. Kira had turned her nanites back on a few times, and they let her know that the *Arbiter* was already in orbit.

Kira had warned Brendan to hold still and wait for her to explain who she was and why the signal had been sent from his cabin. Noting that the pair wore Offense bracers beneath their long-sleeved shirts made her glad for that. They were security.

The first to enter the room was a dark-haired woman with amber skin and pale gray eyes. She was followed by an extremely tall man with blond hair, blue eyes and...

"Khel?" Kira sat up straighter.

"Kira…"

Khel nodded curtly, his stance relaxing. "Stand down, Sorca. She's with us."

"Actually, she's with me," Brendan stood and crossed his arms, glaring at Khel.

Kira couldn't help but laugh at the obvious claim Brendan was staking. It wasn't just that he was half Khel's mass. From what she'd heard, Khel had always been averse to using *Coupling* even by himself, let alone with a partner. Genetically he might be a glitch, but he acted like a perfect Sadirian soldier. Her laughter cut off abruptly as General Serath walked into the room.

His hair was dark and reached the collar of his shirt. His face was half-covered by what looked like the start of a beard. That was a change from the images she'd seen. But it was definitely Serath. One eye was as green as the sunsets on Vega-3, the other blue as the sky outside.

She leapt to her feet, fighting to extract herself from the quilt. It dropped to the ground as she stood at attention. In her periphery, she saw Brendan salute.

Her stomach knotted. Why was General Serath planetside?

He stepped aside, revealing a tiny woman with blonde hair pulled back in a ponytail and huge glasses resting on her small nose. An Earthling?

As if that wasn't confusing enough, the woman reached for General Serath's hand…and he let her take it.

The room spun a bit as Kira's sense of reality adjusted to the new data. Apparently, she wasn't the only one who had fallen for an Earthling.

"Report."

General Serath's order snapped her into her role as a Coalition soldier. *Don't think. Just obey.*

"Sir. Two Tau Cetis detected our broadcast. They've been neutralized."

Kira nodded briefly to the two bound and drugged Tau Cetis in the corner of the cabin. Sorca and Khel were already securing them with Coalition tech. Kira relaxed a bit, glad to have suspension disks to back up the *Balance* still in their systems.

"Good work," General Serath said.

"Sir?" Kira could feel her eyes bugging out of her head. Good work? It was just her duty. Why would he praise her for that? The blonde woman smiled and shifted closer.

Cygnus X...

This time, he caught Kira's stare and grimaced. "And?"

Kira cleared her throat. "We've determined that the Planetary Liaison had falsified my assignment to get me on the listening station so that he could scrub the reports before sending them to the Coalition."

"And where is the listening station?"

Moons. She stood straighter. "Destroyed, sir. It was boarded by the Tau Ceti. I initiated a self-destruct in an attempt to disable their ship and take out as many as I could while preventing them from obtaining the data they sought."

Please, let them never find out how…

"You did more than disable their ship," Sorca said. She had a grin that was nothing less than bloodthirsty. It somehow made Kira like the woman. "You destroyed it. We scanned the debris field."

Kira nodded, her stomach tight. Taking out a Tau Ceti vessel wasn't an easy feat. She had done it with a *listening station*. An odd emotion bubbled up inside of her. Was this what pride felt like?

General Serath was staring at her. She tried not to fidget.

"We also have obtained additional information," she said.

"We?"

Her stomach seemed to drop through the floor. "I was assisted by—"

"Brendan Sloan."

Brendan held up his hand, splitting his fingers in a "V" shape again. She'd have to ask him about that later—if they had a 'later'.

The woman at General Serath's side laughed and returned the gesture.

"I knew I recognized a fellow nerd," Brendan said.

"And proud of it. I'm Evelyn Chambers."

"Very pleased to meet you."

"Since Earth has different customs with introductions,

allow me," Evelyn said. "The big blond guy is Khel, second-in-command of the *Arbiter*, which is this totally amazing spaceship. That's Sorca, head of security. And this is General Serath, but on Earth, he goes by Adam Smith."

General Serath grimaced, but nodded to confirm her statement.

"Ma'am. Aliens." Brendan tapped his forehead twice in an odd gesture that made him seem he was wearing an invisible hat.

Evelyn grinned again.

He nodded toward Kira and said, "Kira made contact after her station was destroyed. She explained that she'd been monitoring a transmission I was sending into deep space and knew I had equipment that could help."

Her stomach filled with butterflies. He was protecting her again. It just might be possible that she would get out of this with all her secrets intact—talking to Brendan, her aberration, falling for an Earthling.

But she didn't want to get away with it. She wanted to stay.

"Sir—"

Everyone in the room turned to her when she didn't continue. She wasn't used to being at the center of so much attention. She took a deep breath and let it out slowly as she took Brendan's hand.

"That's only part of what happened."

Khel let out a chuff of breath and stalked to the door,

leaning against the wall next to it. Sorca's eyes widened, but that grin came back.

The General—Adam—scowled.

Kira could feel her heartbeat in her throat. Adam was very likely to order a mind-wipe for Brendan. It was protocol. Being free or being in prison didn't really matter at that point. Either way, she would have lost the most important part of her life—Brendan's love.

"Permission to speak freely, sir?"

Evelyn jabbed Adam in the rib, hard. He let out a little grunt, then sighed. "I'm going to regret this. Permission granted."

Speaking her mind to one of the greatest Generals the Coalition had ever seen. Kira wasn't sure what to say, how to begin.

Brendan squeezed her hand. She looked up into his eyes, brimming with warmth and love.

"Tell him." Brendan shrugged. "Just tell him."

She took a deep breath and stared at the ground for a moment while she collected herself. "I didn't excel at anything in the pod where I was raised. I didn't...suck." She smiled at Brendan, and he smiled back. Just that simple act was infinitely reassuring. "But I didn't have anything anyone was looking for. That's why they put a nanNet in me. To make me good for something."

She felt Brendan's grip tighten, could sense the tension coming off of him. And she knew in that moment that he still would have fallen in love with her just as she was. He would have accepted her—cherished her—without trying to change her. How could she possibly let go of this?

"I thought it would finally mean a good assignment. A ship, a crew. Colleagues. Friends."

Pain rose up from her gut, strong as a gravity well. It pulled at her, trying to draw out her hope, to crush her with the weight of the memories of loneliness. She wouldn't let it.

"Instead, they put me in a listening station. Single-unit orbiters. I have the data storage, why not. And it turned out, I was good at it. I *am* good at it. Listening. So they kept me on assignments. For four years I have been alone, orbiting worlds with sentient beings as alien to me as…" She shook her head. "As the people who raised me."

"That's not protocol," Khel said. "You should have been assigned rest-cycles for months between assignments."

"When has protocol stopped anyone from doing something that's easy?" Kira said. "I didn't speak up. I accepted the assignments, one after another, because I wanted to feel useful. I wanted to help. And then, I heard Brendan. And…I broke protocol myself. I answered him. But I had to." She looked pointedly at Adam's hand, gripping Evelyn's tight. "You of all people have to understand what it's like to finally find that person you can connect to on a…*human* level. How can I let that go, sir? Could you?"

"What are you suggesting?" Adam asked.

"I want to stay." She was surprised and gratified at how strong her voice sounded. Inside, she was shaking.

"You know what this means."

Kira wasn't sure she had heard him correctly. Was he actually thinking about letting her stay?

"Revoking your citizenship," he said. "Never being allowed to leave the planet."

She could handle that. "Yes, sir."

"And having your nanNet permanently disabled."

Her heart seized. For a normal augmented person, they might be upset to lose the extra functionality. For her, it meant losing the only companions she'd had during her long years of isolation. Before Brendan.

"No," Brendan said. "No freaking way. You're not taking that from her."

She squeezed his hand to warn him. It wouldn't make sense for her to be too upset about it. She had explained her aberration to Brendan while they waited for the *Arbiter* to return, including the danger of others finding out about it.

"It's protocol," Adam said.

"Protocol would be to give the Earthling a mind-wipe and throw Kira in jail." Everyone turned to Sorca. She shrugged one shoulder, then grinned. "I've never been a fan of protocol."

Brendan gestured to Sorca. "What she said. I'm not getting a mind-wipe, whatever that is, and Kira's keeping her nanNet. And her citizenship."

Adam arched an eyebrow.

"I'm not asking your permission to play *Little House on the Ignorant Prairie*." He turned to Kira and said, "This isn't just about us."

Right. Kira nodded. "The Tau Ceti aren't just setting up pockets of their habitat on Earth. They're feeding on Earthlings."

"What?" Evelyn stepped forward, glancing to Adam.

"Those guys on the floor?" Brendan said. "They're vampire space frogs."

Evelyn laughed until she noted Brendan didn't join her. "Oh, you're serious."

Adam wrapped his arm around her as she shifted closer.

"They're siphoning off oxytocin and other hormones from humans," Kira said.

"So they get a hit like Coalition citizens and *Balance*." Sorca flinched ever so slightly, glancing at the other soldiers. When she and Kira met gazes again, she knew Kira had picked up on the hidden data in her statement. Kira could see the nervousness in Sorca's eyes. Sorca didn't use *Balance*, either.

"Don't get me started on that," Brendan said. "I've learned enough about your government to have serious concerns about you making decisions for my homeworld. It ends now."

"What are you suggesting?" Adam said.

"I'm not suggesting anything. It's done." Brendan wrapped his arm around Kira's waist, mirroring Adam's posture with Evelyn. "I don't care what the Coalition thinks about Earth's level of development. We're forming the committee for pre-First Contact work. The Department of Homeworld Security. You want to make a decision about my people, you're going to talk to us first."

"I see Kira has explained quite a bit about our society." Adam fixed her with an uncomfortable stare. "But she seems to have neglected to inform you that you're not in the position to make demands."

"Oh, she didn't have to. I inferred from what she told me and set up some things while she was out of the room."

"What did you do?" Kira's heart sank. She had only left the room for a few minutes to use the bathroom. What could Brendan have set up in that time?

"I'm sorry I didn't talk to you about it first, but I wanted you to have plausible deniability."

Sorca said, "I doubt an Earthling has the resources to do anything that could possibly impact the Coalition."

"I guess I forgot to mention that I work with my own government," Brendan said. "And while I agree that they aren't ready to handle all this alien stuff, there are a few of us that can pool our resources and help to guide the Coalition into making better choices for our planet."

"Such as?"

"Like making Kira the planetary liaison."

Kira's stomach lurched. Brendan hadn't mentioned this when they talked before.

"I'm not going to tell you what I've done, because it'd make it that much easier for you to try to stop me. Frankly, though, I'd rather we work together. These space vampires are feeding on my people and destroying our ecosystems. That has to stop."

"Agreed," Evelyn said.

Adam nodded. "Agreed."

Kira thought Adam was only referring to their goals, but then he said, "Kira will be the new planetary liaison for Earth. I'll see to it."

Kira felt her jaw drop. Her gaze met Evelyn's and the Earthling smiled so warmly that Kira couldn't stop herself from returning it.

She was going to be Earth's next planetary liaison… She could stay with Brendan, help protect his homeworld. Finally, she could make a difference. And she wouldn't be alone.

"One last matter," Brendan said. "My sister might be in the line of fire. She's an environmental scientist whose work is somehow tying her in with the ecosystems the Tau Ceti are messing with. I want a bodyguard for her. Someone who can stand up to space frogs."

Adam nodded. "Khel."

"No no no. I am not sending Thor here to watch over my baby sister." He glared and Khel and said, "Kira, *please* tell me this isn't one of the guys you used *Coupling* with."

Khel looked shocked for a moment, then launched himself at Brendan. Luckily both the couch and Adam were in his way. Adam grabbed Khel and pulled him back as Kira stepped in front of Brendan. The revulsion on Khel's face was unmistakable.

"I've never used *Coupling* in my life!" Khel said.

"He didn't understand the insult," Kira said. She tried to keep her voice level.

Brendan's eyebrows hitched up his forehead, then he grinned. "My bad. I take it back. This guy's the perfect bodyguard for Paige."

There was a moment of awkward silence, then Evelyn laughed. When everyone turned to her, she shrugged. "I was just thinking, Kira's going to be living on Earth now. That makes her a resident alien."

Brendan laughed, then turned to Kira and kissed her, passionately—in front of everyone.

"Welcome to Earth," he said.

Epilogue

This planet was vexing. Khel walked along the sidewalk observing the Earthlings scattered about the area.

According to his cultural indoctrination session, those walking the same direction as him were supposed to stay on his right, while those walking toward him belonged on his left. An alarming number of humans chose to weave in and out of the pedestrian traffic, sometimes even stepping into the area reserved for use by vehicles to get around others.

Chaos.

And this was the sort of free-will that General Serath—Adam—wanted to bring to the Coalition? As Khel watched, an Earthling darted in front of an automobile, barely escaping injury. The human operating the vehicle pounded on the steering wheel, causing it to emit an ear-splitting alarm. Khel paused to cover his ears and someone ran into his back.

"Watch it, buddy." The Earthling scuttled around Khel, lifting the middle finger of one hand and pointing it at him.

Khel didn't remember that gesture from the cultural indoctrination session he'd received from Vay aboard the

Arbiter. He lifted his own middle finger of the same hand, pointing it at the human, and said, "Excuse me."

The Earthling scowled, then quickened his pace.

The sooner Khel could complete his mission and leave this bewildering planet, the better. He turned a corner, thankfully onto a less populated sidewalk. A large building dominated the area, a cut-out image of a severed arm with grotesquely bulging muscles hanging over its door.

He ran his hand over the muscles of his own arm— exposed, thanks to the Earth-style "T-shirt" he wore instead of his uniform. The stylized rendering of the arm above him was similar to his own freakish level of musculature. But why wasn't it depicted as being attached to a body?

Khel suppressed a chill. *What is this place?*

He steeled his nerves, then pulled open the door and stepped inside.

The scent struck him first, making him recoil and shake his head. He wasn't sure how to describe it, other than acrid and *stale.*

There was no one guarding the entrance, so he quickly made his way through the entry chamber, heading toward an open archway on his right. He could hear movement from within, strained grunts and the clanging of metal on metal.

The archway opened up to a large room filled with strange equipment. Some had benches or stools, as if people were supposed to sit on them. Perhaps it was some sort of interrogation area?

He turned toward the grunting noise he'd heard, only to see a prone Earthling on one of the benches, holding a metal bar above his chest. The bar had metal discs attached to each end. From the way the man's muscles pulled and the beads of sweat coating his body, it must be extremely heavy.

The bar started to drop. Khel took a step forward, intending to prevent the human from being crushed, but before the bar hit the man's chest, he pushed it back up, holding it in the air above him. As Khel watched, the human repeated the movement several times. He then set the bar onto a metal rack above his head.

The activity made no sense.

Another sound drew his attention—this one a steady drone. He gazed out over the room to see a woman with bright red hair standing on one of the pieces of equipment. She should have caught his eye immediately, but he'd been too focused on the disturbing sounds of the human closer to him.

Khel brought himself back to task. He was here on a mission, and he was fairly certain he'd just found his target. She was walking on a conveyer belt that continually moved beneath her feet. Perpetual motion with no destination. Her eyes were fixed on the blank wall opposite her with a single-minded focus that completely baffled him. What was she even looking at?

This place must be a test of one's sanity. The whole planet was beginning to feel that way to Khel. His training might not be sufficient to protect him for long. He needed to retrieve his target and get them both out of there as quickly as possible—back to the *Arbiter*.

He may have found her first, but he doubted his enemies were far behind. And if the cybernetically enhanced soldiers of Tau Ceti caught up with her before Khel could get her to safety, these odd apparatuses would seem like a recreation facility when they were done with her.

He headed toward his target, intent on one thing, one person only. Paige Sloan.

—

I hope you enjoyed *Resident Alien!* I know you've been waiting for Khel's story and am happy to tell you it's next. I had so much fun learning more about him, as well as the take-charge Earthling that can more than handle him—but not necessarily the affect he has on her. Read on for a sneak peek at *Business or Pleasure.*

Business or Pleasure

The Department of Homeworld Security
Book Three

Chapter One

At six-thirty on Saturday mornings, the gym was usually deserted. It was therefore Paige's favorite workout of the week. She had already completed a few circuits on the weight machines and was enjoying being the only person using the line of treadmills as she cooled down. After the week she'd had, she needed the break from human contact.

Her playlist abruptly switched to her brother Brendan's ringtone. Damn.

Thanks to him, all she had to do to answer was tap her

right earbud. He had hooked her up with technology he'd designed himself. The earbuds included tiny microphones that could pick up her voice even if she was whispering, while filtering out ambient noise and making her hands-free talking crystal clear. The phone's reception was good enough that she wondered if he was tapping into one of the secret government satellites he worked on.

Allegedly.

The downside of the awesome tech was that she felt obligated to answer every time he called her with it. She sighed, then tapped the earbud.

"Morning, bro. What's up?"

"Hey. You're at the gym, right?"

She hesitated before answering. "Yeah."

"I figured. How are you doing?"

"I'm fine, everything is fine…"

Except it really wasn't. Jim—Senator Conroy—was dead. Today's workout was as much about grief and catharsis as keeping up with her physical health. She wasn't just sad to lose the best boss she'd ever had. Senator Conroy had been a passionate visionary. He was determined to tighten environmental laws.

Her team, which consisted of her and two ever-changing temporary interns from the local college, had been working several sites in Louisiana for three years before Jim came on board, giving her renewed hope that she could make a difference. He had been in office less than a month when his plane crashed.

Maybe Brendan was just calling to check up on her.

"I'm sending someone over," he said.

She let out another sigh, deeper than the first. "Seriously? We're not even in the same state."

"I have a...friend in the area," he said. "He should be there any minute."

"How do you even know what gym I'm at?"

"Uh..."

"Don't bother answering."

Brendan was overprotective to the point of paranoia. She had finally been able to get him to stop hiring and assigning her bodyguards by agreeing to carry a panic button with her at all times. Brendan had designed it to look like lipstick. She wasn't sure how it worked—she just knew to press the button and it would send him some sort of signal that let him know where she was and that she was in trouble.

"I've told you before, I refuse to let your work impact my life. You want to work on top secret stuff—"

"Paige—"

"—that's your business. But I'm not going to walk around with ex-military private security goons following me just to make you feel better about your life choices."

"Paige!"

Brendan never yelled. She stopped ranting.

"This isn't about me or my work," he said. "It's about you."

"What about me?"

"Whatever you're working on has caught the attention of…unsavory types."

She let out a brief laugh. "I can't even get people to believe global climate change is real, let alone that it's impacting key ecosystems. I doubt anybody sees my work as a threat, especially now that Senator Conroy is gone."

"I wish that was the case. Listen to me very carefully. I can't speak openly right now."

She snorted. Right, Brendan couldn't speak openly on the incredibly advanced, encoded system that he had designed. She was pretty sure the government would be pissed if they ever found out she was walking around with the tech he had given her. Brendan had assured her when he set her up with her phone and panic button that no one would know about it and his *gifts* wouldn't pose a threat to national security. The last thing she wanted was to be walking around with classified technology.

As rudimentary as he claimed it to be, her calls were still supposed to be one-hundred percent unhackable. If Brendan couldn't talk freely, that meant either he had been pulled back in by the government and they were eavesdropping using the tech he had designed for them, or the much more terrifying possibility—someone was with him that Brendan deemed a threat.

"You don't need a wormhole, do you?"

That was their code for a dangerous situation they

needed a miracle to get out of—like the sudden appearance of a stable wormhole. His answer would let her know if he was safe. He laughed, and some of the tension in her chest receded.

"Not in the sense you mean. You wouldn't believe... Well, anyway, I'm in a safe spot. And I'm sending someone to bring you here. We need to talk."

"I'm glad you're safe, but I'm not leaving."

"Paige—"

"If I'm on someone's radar, that means I'm onto something. I'm not about to drop it." Whatever *it* was.

Most people would consider her overworked, but she didn't care about the long hours. She was dedicated to helping the planet. The problem with the heavy workload was that she had so many locations and projects she was tracking, she had no clue which one had pushed someone's buttons.

Brendan's call had spooked her though. She glanced around the gym, noting that several people had filtered in while they spoke. Everyone seemed absorbed in their workouts.

"I'm not telling you to abandon your work," Brendan said. "I'm saying there's more going on here than you realize. Much more. You're going to need help, whether you want it or not."

"I don't want one of your..."

A tall man stepped into the main workout room. He was

pale and blond, his hair cut short on the sides and back with bangs that fell partway down his forehead. His gray T-shirt pulled tight across the most gorgeous pecs she had ever seen. His broad shoulders perfectly offset his narrow hips and accented his V figure. Tight jeans encased his long legs, all the way down to…black boots.

She rolled her eyes. He might have been able to fool her if not for the boots. Well, and the stance. The way he walked screamed military. The question at the front of her mind became—was he Brendan's guy or someone else's?

"Tell me more about this friend you're sending."

"He's tall. Looks like Thor. Not like movie-Thor, but actual *God of Lighting*-Thor."

She grinned. "And you felt safe sending him to watch over your baby sister?"

Before Brendan had made her the panic button, Paige had seduced a few of the more attractive bodyguards he tried to saddle her with. It was a great way to let off steam, but invariably had led to them wanting more of a commitment. She was already committed to her work. Still, it worked for getting them to quit and gave her fuel to tease her brother.

"Please try to take this seriously. Khel will keep you safe and explain as much as he can."

"Kel?"

"K-H-E-L. Go easy on him. He's not from around here."

"I'll make sure he feels welcome." She purred the

words, wanting to make Brendan uncomfortable. He should be for intruding in her life this way—again.

"Yeah, good luck with that. And gross." Brendan laughed as if he knew something she didn't. Which wasn't that unusual. He was quiet for a moment, then said, "I love you, sis."

"I love you, too. Be safe."

"And you."

She tapped the earbud to end the call, then turned off her music. That had been their standard wrap up to a conversation, but there was a new tension to it. The teasing had been more strained, and that pause before his, 'I love you...'

She tried to shake off the unease and focused instead on the hottie headed her way. This guy might be enough for her to chance a fling. Her body was already tingling just from watching him approach. He was scanning the room, his brows drawn together so tight they almost touched in the center of his forehead. When he reached her, he stared at her legs.

Okay, he was a leg guy. After a few moments longer than a normal person would stare, he cleared his throat and said, "Paige Sloan. I am Khel."

He cut himself off, as if he was used to saying something more than that. Probably rank and serial number.

"Khel. I am Paige Sloan," she parroted back. He didn't pick up on the teasing. If anything, he seemed reassured by her mocking response.

"Your brother has sent me to secure your safety. We must leave at once."

"My brother is not in charge of me. Nor are you. We will leave when I'm good and ready."

His mouth dropped open, then shut, then opened, then shut. Like a giant thunder-god goldfish.

She laughed. He scowled.

Right, she was supposed to take it easy on him.

"I'm almost done with my workout. Surely the world won't end if I spend another minute on the treadmill."

He stared at her feet, then looked back over the room. She thought he was checking for threats again, but then he said, "What are you all doing?"

"We're working out."

The treadmill beeped and she hit the button to turn it off. He glanced back at her as she jumped down and grabbed her towel. She felt a bead of sweat run between her cleavage and noticed how his gaze followed it. She blotted at her neck as she stepped in close.

Standing on the floor instead of the treadmill, he was even taller than she thought. She had to crane her neck back to look at him. He had that same confused scowl on his face.

"You know," she said. "Exercise?"

Nothing.

She gestured to his physique. "How do you stay in such

great shape?"

"Now is not the time for questions," he said.

Eyeing him up and down, she made her voice breathy as she said, "Then I guess you can leave it to my imagination."

His gaze snapped back to hers and his lips thinned as he pressed them together. She turned and headed for the locker room, grinning as he fell in step behind her.

"We must leave at once," he said.

"Not until I shower." She pulled out her earbuds and tucked them into the back pocket of her workout shorts next to her phone.

"This *shower* can not be more important than your safety. The longer we delay, the more opportunities our enemies will have to attack."

He sounded like one of Brendan's cosplaying friends. For a moment, she wondered if the whole thing was an elaborate charade.

"If this is Brendan playing a practical joke on me, I'm going to kick his ass when I see him."

"That is outside the scope of my orders."

She rolled her eyes and pushed open the door to the women's locker room. Khel followed her in.

"Um, Khel?"

"Yes?"

He stopped when she did, glancing around the room. If this *was* a joke, he was taking it pretty seriously. He also didn't seem disturbed at all at being in a women's locker room.

"You're not supposed to be in here," she said.

"I go where you go."

He fixed his gaze on her, clear blue eyes boring through her. She decided to have a little fun.

"Okay."

She gripped the bottom of her sports bra—the only top she wore while working out—and pulled it over her head, smirking. His gaze flicked to her chest, then back to her face. He didn't even look like he was *trying* not to look.

She wasn't used to men ignoring her body. She worked hard to be attractive. It helped her self-esteem and prevented her from having to endure lonely nights when she felt like a little company. She was *stacked* and never had trouble finding men who considered the red hair and blue eyes a bonus.

Khel didn't flinch, didn't twitch, didn't alter his expression or body language one iota. He just stared at her. At her *face*.

"Proceed," he said.

Wow. That pinged her ego. She turned around and walked to her locker.

Whatever. He wasn't into her. It had happened before and would happen again. She had to admit she was disappointed, though. He was gorgeous and it had been a while since she'd indulged in a carnal weekend with anyone.

She finished stripping and threw her workout clothes into a bag, then grabbed her toiletries and slid on some flip-flops. Khel stood at the end of the row of lockers, looking left and right. Good thing the locker room was empty.

As she walked past him to the showers, he started after her. The thought of him watching her shower with that cold stare set her teeth on edge.

"Not so fast." She turned around and planted a hand on his chest.

Heat and warmth flooded into her. His chest was rock-hard, and damn, those shoulders. She could grab onto them and do all sorts of things...

Khel sucked in a huge breath and held it. Okay. That was a response. But she wasn't into mixed signals. She pulled her hand away.

"This is as far as you go," she said.

"I am ordered to see to your safety."

"I don't care what my brother says."

He bristled. "I don't take orders from a...Brendan."

A Brendan?

She finished his original sentence in her head. *He doesn't take orders from a civilian.*

Shit. Khel was military, but not 'ex'. Brendan had told her he was taking a break from his projects. He must have been pulled back in—and somehow she was swept up with it.

Yes, technically they both worked for the government, and yes, she had received a certain level of clearance based on whatever the hell he was working on. But she had her own life, her own job, her own cause.

She would not be controlled.

—

About the Author

USA Today Bestselling author Cassandra Chandler uses her vivid imagination to make the world more interesting, spawning the ideas she turns into her whimsical Science Fiction romcoms and darkly evocative Paranormal and Urban Fantasy Romances. Fast-paced and funny, lighthearted or dark, her stories will introduce you to characters you want to be friends with and worlds where you'd like to build a vacation home.